LANAYRE LIGGERA

INTRUSION

INTRUSION

CHAPTER 1

"All rise! All rise!"

Luncheon being over, Sir Carter Braxton closed his chamber door behind him, and mounted the bench in his red, black, and white judge's robe and wig. The only judges to keep their colored robes were in the criminal division, and were colored red, the color of blood.

Next, he extracted his wire-rimmed reading glasses to scan his notes, then glanced over to the prosecution, the defense, and the twelve -person jury, without making any direct eye contact. His last glance was over the spectators.

Just as the door was to be closed, a middle-aged woman, her auburn hair held up by a unique silver hair clasp, missed being shut out by seconds. Whoever she was, she made the judge start. He scribbled a note for the clerk to deliver to her on which he had written, 'tea after, my chambers?' and watched as curious eyes followed the path of the clerk to the back of the room. He hoped he had not embarrassed either of them.

He saw her scribble something very short, and hand it back to the clerk, who returned it to the judge, again, with curiosity in the eyes of the audience and the legal representatives. By this time, however, the judge's face resumed its judicial lack of personal expression, and when he spoke, it was with his public voice.

The woman had not expected high security—ID, purse search, metal detector, even having her hair let down to check for concealed explosives. "Don't be offended, Ma'am, it would be the same if you were wearing a turban."

The trial finished with the prosecutor's and defense's last plea to the jury. After both pleas, the judge gave his instructions to the jury, while the woman watched with clear interest in the proceedings.

She surveyed the judge. He still had a sharp profile and clean features— time had treated him gently for a man nearing fifty. The few lines in his face that occurred were gently etched, while hair that escaped from under his wig was still brown.

The jury was ushered out of the room, with the usual noise of chairs scraping, footfalls, coughs, and whispers. The spectators left until the call for the jury to return to pronounce the verdict. The woman noticed there were still what seemed to be an unusual number of security personnel still in the room.

The judge left the bench, walking toward her. She had never seen him in full judge's regalia before, and it was awe-inspiring; a white wing collar and bands and a white wig, a black stole and belt, a swag of red that that crossed his chest from his shoulder to his waist, and, at the ends of his sleeves, a wrap of blue- grey protective material to keep the red fabric from rubbing on the bench.

"Valerie," he said. "How very nice to see you. Are you staying in London?"

"Only for the weekend, for a visit with our solicitor. I thought I'd duck in to see if you were around."

"Shall we have some tea until the jury returns?"

"That would be delightful."

"Give me just one moment." He walked over to another man— who was the court reporter, and they spoke for a few minutes.

He returned and offered her his arm, which she took. They emerged into the hallway. He guided her to his chambers, where his clerk, Ms. T., prepared the tea.

"Valerie, please sit down," he said, indicating an armchair beside the couch, with a table fronting it.

Now, he removed his bench wig, different than the one he had worn when last she saw him when he was still a barrister in silks. She was pleased to see he was not losing his hair, a hard experience for men.

He handed his wig to his clerk and she put it in its box. Then he reached to the back of his neck, where a gold stud and white and black string ties kept the wing collar and bands and the black stole over his robe in place. He asked his clerk to undo the black string and took off the stole and belt, but kept the white one in place that held his wing collar and bands. He undid his black belt which anchored the red swag over his shoulder and crossed his chest diagonally; his clerk helped him out of his robe and hung it up. On the rack were also a winter robe with fur (which made him feel a bit like Santa Claus) and a black jacket for pre-trial motions. He put on his suit jacket. As usual, there was a plain brown tie hung over his desk chair, the same color as his suit and waistcoat, as he was partially color blind. She felt he was more familiar now that he had doffed his regalia. He sat down on the couch next to her chair, and MsT. served the tea.

She gazed around her.

Strange things were juxtaposed in chambers. Behind his desk chair was an oil painting, a portrait of an unknown judge, and beside it, a panel labelled, 'Personal Attack Alarm'. White file cabinets were all neatly closed. Bookcases lined the walls, containing a gamut of sets of books bound in bright red, bright blue, and bright green, intermixed with older sets with a dull blue gray binding and a red band near the top with the title. A smattering of individual volumes finished the content. By the door, a sign boasted 'Emergency Procedures.' Bottles of liquor sat atop a small floor bookcase. A floor radiator, a lamp sitting on the seat of a green upholstered chair, and paper piled in boxes in neat piles scattered everywhere completed the contents of his chambers. In the center of the room was a beige upholstered sofa, with matching armchairs at either end.

The woman was slightly paralyzed with discomfort. How had she ever gotten herself into such a sophisticated place?

"I will be in the outer office, Judge," his clerk said.

"Very good, Ms. T."

He stood up again, and moved to his desk, where he picked up a blue telephone and said, "One person in chambers with me, Mrs. Valerie Falconer, Pendragon, Forest of Dean." He turned to her. "I beg your pardon, Valerie, but I am living under tight security." The woman wondered who he was talking to. He sat down on the couch again.

"I was—I admit—wondering what happened to you, especially—" she said and stopped awkwardly.

"Yes, I know. I was not to contact any friends, as it might put them at risk. Believe me, that was an awful day. I did find a way to contact you every year, via Adry."

"Yes."

And how is my little god daughter?"

"We've all had—some major readjustments."

"May I inquire why you are meeting with your solicitor? You need not answer if I am intruding, but we have a few instructing solicitors who aid the criminal court." He understood that at this point in time, to become involved would only induce more complications. Still, he had to ask. And she had to answer.

"Do you recall—you may not—some years ago, you undertook to vet our business records one weekend, and Adry sat with you while you explained what you could find out to him? Although he was a child, he carried away the impression you did not consider that his grandparents had upped the prices enough, but that his father was planning to leave things as they were until his parents either got out of the business entirely or predeceased him?"

The judge thought a moment. "I believe I do."

"With his parents gone, came the inheritance tax. Then Adrian died of a stroke, and there was another inheritance tax. That is why Adry decided to go to London School of Economics. He was afraid we might be forced into bankruptcy."

"Lord, yes."

Now they were on more familiar turf, and the awkwardness dissipated.

"Wouldn't your family float you a loan?"

"Why throw good money over bad? Even if we recovered the property, we had no one to run the business."

Ah, yes, the entrepreneurial Herringtons, thought the judge.

Ms. T. knocked and entered, "Jury has returned, judge," she said.

"Blimey! I thought they would debate it longer."

With amazing quickness, he stripped off his suit jacket and waistcoat, and his clerk helped him back into his robe.

"Valerie, you may stay in chambers if you wish, this won't take long."

"Oh, no, I am curious to see the end of a trial," she replied. From her body language, he was quite sure she would dine with Adry tonight and begin to sort things out.

Her reply was affirmative. "Then I plan to find a way to relax tomorrow," she added. "Do you have any suggestions, Carter?"

"I am preprogrammed, Valerie. On Saturday I do something the British public rather frowns on. I practice at my gun club. I'm not sure that would be to your taste."

"Oh, for God's sake, Carter—I'm from Texas!'

"Where are you staying?"

She told him.

"I shall come for you at nine-thirty if that is agreeable."

CHAPTER 2

It was ten o'clock on a Saturday morning. Carter drove his Range Rover at eighty-five miles per hour, between two police escorts.

"The less time on the road, the less exposure," he explained, as he broke the speed limit. "This is the only time I get to drive my own car." One brown- booted foot pressed the accelerator, matched by brown corduroy pants and a white turtle neck sweater. *It seems he can discern between lighter and heavier colors,* she noticed.

Now it was a bit strange for her, as they had rarely sat together without Adrian.

"How is my little god daughter, Mercy?" he asked.

"I noticed you had a picture of her on your desk."

"It will be the only picture of children I shall ever have!"

What's the answer to that one. "Can we ever be so sure of things?" she asked.

"Moderately. There is one thing I do hope to be able to do, which is to visit Adrian's gravesite."

The first escort car turned off the road, pulling to a stop. Then the second police escort behind him also stopped. A policeman got out, and walked over to them; Carter unlocked the car, and the man took command of a back seat.

In front of them lay a muddy road filled with bumps and dips, something which would make one glad to have a Range Rover. Putting the car in low gear, Carter tortuously wound down the road, hitting bottom only once. In the silence, Valerie turned backward, and said to the bobby, "Valerie Falconer."

"Pleased to meet you, Madame. Sergeant Harry Post."

Carter stopped at a gate marked TG, signaling Sgt. Post to get out and open it, then drove through. The Sergeant closed and locked the gate behind them.

As they moved forward, Valerie inquired uneasily, "Aren't we supposed to wait for the policeman?" Carter swiftly stamped down on the brake without a word. *Um oh, I've butted in again.* She had violated unspoken British class behavior. "Sorry, Carter," she remarked.

"I do forget you are an American," he replied, with smile.

"What is this?" Valerie asked, as in front of them stood three high walls of rock, like three quarters of a giant box.

"An old quarry, "Carter replied. "There are rust-colored indentations at regular intervals, where they drilled to insert explosives to blow off a new layer of rock face."

"Rotten thing to be a blaster," remarked the returned Sergeant, "I had a mate who was a blaster. He jumped behind a protective wall before he exploded the blast. After a while, it took whiskey in the morning to keep him going, and one day, he didn't step behind the wall."

"I'll wager his parts are still coming down," said Carter brusquely.

Clearly, he doesn't consider it proper for his bodyguard to insert himself into a conversation. I still get things wrong after growing up in a democracy.

Valerie always packed one pair of white Levis into the bottom of her suitcase just in case. Today her foresight paid off. When Carter asked her to sign in, she was aware that the people behind her heard her American accent. *Bloody hell.*

"I don't do the Wild West or the American Constitution anymore, Carter," she whispered.

They had reached Carter's shooting station. At his feet was his carrying box, with two .22 Browning pistols and a Colt Navy 1851 reproduction revolver. He began to load the target pistol, put a clip in the butt, pushing the slide, which cocked the hammer, then, released the slide which pushed the bullet into the chamber. "Fire!" said the microphone. Valerie watched his shooting stance. It was good and all his shots landed in the middle of the target.

He probably would do better if I weren't watching him.

He loaded the second pistol and handed it to her. *Doesn't want me loading it—afraid I'll muck it up.* "Come on Valerie, give it a try." She stepped up to the shooting station and without hesitation, took the pistol. She fired off the clip. "Splatter shot!" she exclaimed with annoyance. Once again, all the magazines popped open, signifying the weapons were out of ammunition. The microphone said, "Arms down." They walked to the target. "The only good thing is that I got a pattern!!" she said, with exasperation. "Can I try again?"

At the next target butt, a man said, "Watch out, old boy! Women who like to shoot are hell on straying husbands!"

Again, Carter was annoyed at the interruption—even as he realized that his weekdays were spent in a situation in which his locutions were paramount, with no interruptions—but he was completely unprepared when Valerie retorted, "You seem to know a bit too much about straying husbands, Mr…"

"Foster. Steve Foster."

"Valerie Falconer, Mr. Foster." She extended her hand.

Hmmm. That's not the Valerie I thought I knew!

Lunch was announced; it was fish and chips.

"After lunch is black powder. Would you like to try?"

"I'll try anything labeled C-O-L- T."

With interest, she watched him rotate the cylinders, load each of the six barrels by pouring a measure of powder, pour in some kind of bird seed to bring up the level up to where the ball should rest in each chamber, and, using a small ramrod to push it all down, covered the tops of the bullets in each barrel with Vaseline. He put a cap over each nipple, then handed it to her just as the speaker commanded, "Fire!" All around her, a volley of shots filled the target range with clouds of smoke. *Ah! The fog of war,"* she noted.

He loaded it again then shot himself.

"I never would have expected you to be a gun enthusiast," she remarked.

"It's easier than learning fencing. They have room for that at court."

"I see."

On the ride home she said, "I haven't enjoyed a day like this in some time!"

"Nor I," he replied. "I've learned not to mention shooting. Are you free for dinner?"

"I can be," she said. "But I must call Adry."

"Shall I drop you at the hotel, then, and come back for you?"

"Oh, that's nice but it's trouble—I'll take a cab."

"Valerie, I shall have to come for you. I'll explain when we get there."

"Oh."

"What time is good?"

"Six thirty? Seven?"

"Six thirty."

Once in her room, Valerie rang Adry. "Adry—Mum—I'm having dinner tonight with Carter Braxton."

"Him?"

"Yes, apparently he's under guard or something."

"That's crazy."

"Afraid not!"

"I thought he dropped off radar."

"Not exactly. He has a picture of Mercy on his desk—a bit outdated."

"Oh, yeah, that godfather bit."

"I think I may invite him to church with us tomorrow morning."

"Good luck with that!"

"He would come with us when he visited."

"He's a polite man," remarked her son.

"Well, he can be polite again. Quite honestly, he used to visit regularly. I think something has happened. You may not remember—

I'm sure you don't—he visited the week after you were born. But you may remember he is why you are about to graduate LSE."

"I'm not sure I follow—"—

"He went over the books at Pendragon for your father."

"Ah—yes."

"Shall I take him off the dance card?"

"No, Mum, do your worst."

Valerie put the receiver back in place. Then she took a shower, thinking of Adry. *He's a bit huffy because we haven't seen hide nor hair of Carter for three years.*

She donned a dress that was halfway between formal and casual and a pair of flats, combed her hair and put it up again. She always wore a faintly colored lipstick. Down to the lobby to wait. She would prefer to wait there, with people coming and going; Carter had always been rather methodical and she expected him precisely at six thirty.

When he arrived, he told her, "I'm afraid I can't take you to a restaurant. It's part of my security. It's my flat or nowhere."

I wish he'd told me that sooner. Maybe he thought I wouldn't come otherwise.

They slowed at a tall white building. On the ground floor was an international realty office and a bank. Three more stories appeared to be offices, windows unlighted because it was Saturday night; but above them were apartments, and a light had just gone on in a window. At the back of the building was a driveway that dipped down toward a basement, and there was a sign, 'Service Entrance.' He drove down without slowing and as the door came closer, she pressed her foot against the floor, yet suddenly the door opened as a scanner read his license plate. They got out and walked over to an elevator door, where Carter pressed his fingerprints onto a plate.

"I apologize; this is a bit tight. It's part of security It's a private elevator."

"You haven't any stairs?"

"No, I'm afraid in an emergency it's up rather than down; I have a passageway to the roof. There is generally a helicopter there." They were standing close together. *He's still in good shape,* she noted. Standing so close to a man again was no longer an everyday thing.

"Here we go." Reaching over to touch a button, they were catapulted upward, arriving at the top floor. The narrow door to the elevator opened and Carter instructed her to proceed him.

"On the admittedly slender chance a hit man could get into the elevator at the garage, here, the door is only wide enough for one person, and there are cameras in the elevator. This would give me time to grab a revolver."

Here he unlocked his flat.

His dining room ran ninety degrees off the living room, one chair looking more used than the others; it was obviously where he sat to eat. A hallway ran off the living room into the back of the flat, and once again, Valerie would have loved to see the rest, but the British did not have the custom of showing anyone over their dwellings.

In the living room two white sofas faced each other with a small table in between. "Please sit here, Valerie, the other has cat hair." Carter sat down on the other one and, to her surprise, a black longhaired cat appeared and jumped into his lap.

From her angle, liquor battles sparkling on two shelves, with wine below it against the wall, with bottles shut into a small refrigerator behind a glass door.

"Would you care for some champagne?"

"That sounds lovely!"

He's very active. Maybe he's nervous.

"Dulcie, my dear," he said to the cat, "move over a bit, I shall be right back." She smiled an inward wry smile. *I don't recall he was ever sweet on animals.* She watched him extract a bottle from the refrigerator and open it like a connoisseur without the merest pop. He handed Valerie her glass and sat down. "Santé," he said, leaning forward. Valerie clinked his glass with hers. At the sound, Dulcie raised her head, jumped down, and came over to Valerie to sniff her.

"She smells our cats," Valerie said. "How did you get her?"

"Some of my guardian chaps found her outside the building and brought her in asking if I would like to have her. She is good company. When I come 'home' she jumps up on the bureau and watches me take off my necktie."

"They certainly can be good company."

"May I ask how your dinner with came off last night?" She had not told him, but he had guessed it from her body language. "I gathered it was serious? You need not answer if you consider it intrusive."

"I dined with Adry. You are right. I decided to try to sell Pendragon, of necessity. Then, one of Adry's fellow students saw a picture of it in the real estate section of the *Times,* and showed it to Adry. The chap was incredulous that Adry would give up a business and start at the bottom of the ladder at some brokerage. Adry said the picture shocked him! He had just been going along with me.

"However, at about that time, I drew some humorous cartoons, I guess you would call them, having to do with Herrington beef in the U.K. My brother Charlie had them stuck on meat for the U.K. and offered me a cut.   I didn't want it to be a way to help me out, but, as it turns out, it did help sales over here. And it changed me from a passive to an active shareholder, which helped our bills! Adry contacted Inland Revenue and made a deal to pay the taxes off slowly."

Ah, yes, the famous Herrington family again.

"Ergo, we are giving it another try."

"I'm so delighted I need another glass of champagne. You?"

CHAPTER 3

The doorbell of the flat rang.

"Ah," he said, "Dinner is arriving." He opened the door. Then he said something to the delivery man she did not understand, and she realized it was in another language.

"I hope it will be something you enjoy," he told her. The man rolled a kitchen cart in with two dishes under covers, set the table, and lifted the covers to reveal lamb chops, potato, and peas.

Then he left, and Carter seated Valerie. He poured her a glass of Chateauneuf du Pape red wine and dimmed the dining room light. In lower illumination he could see a patina of sorrow on her face, her skin the color of worn porcelain from being out-of-doors.,

"Would you like to join me, Adry, and his girlfriend Brie for church and lunch at Rules?" She asked. "That is, if you can." *I'm beginning to get the hang of this security thing.*

"I'll ring my guardians after supper." And he did. He ran the call through Scotland Yard. A short agreeable conversation ensued, apparently, since he returned to the table with a smile.

"Yes. Church is a random happening, as is Rules. I should very much like to see Adry again, and to meet his current girl. And the Sidi would like to meet this Mrs. Falconer, with whom I have spent the day."

"Who is?"

"My keeper."

"Who is he?"

"He owns the building."

"Am I in for the third degree?"

"That's all taken care of, Valerie. Blue phone, Mrs. Valerie Falconer, Forest of Dean?"

"I see. It's your turn to fill in the past!"

"Without too many particulars, we were considering whether we could hold a trial for a middleman for shipping crude oil, and the Sidi had discovered that this man had a nasty habit of assassinating judges. One day, the Sidi asked our judges to assemble, along with my old mentor, Nate, to ascertain whether we had a judge who would take the case, whose safe-housing might endure for some time. I had asked Nate if I might sit in the back of the room; I was curious. The Sidi looked our judges over and said to Nate, 'No fire in their bellies. They will all recuse themselves. Who is that chap at the back of the room? Is he any good?' Nate replied he had trained me himself."

"Oh—your old professor?"

"The very one."

"How does he deal with mental stress?" the examiners asked.

"Quite well, I'd say," said Nate.

"The Sidi said he would see to my protection. Would you come into my study with me?"

Valerie followed him as he opened the door to one room. Dulcie also followed him. It had red curtains and a lovely Oriental carpet, desks with an electric typewriter, Dictaphone, fax machine, radio, television, and computer, the lockbox required by law for anyone possessing firearms, which separated ammunition from the weapons, and special safety locks required for persons possessing firearms in the residence on the windows.

"You don't keep them at your club?"

"No. Khalil has invented something for me that activates and drops the clip into the section for my revolvers."

The room was completed with three walls of bookcases. In the middle of the room was a deep, cushy- looking sofa. On the wall was a map.

"Here is where my problem used to live," Carter said, pointing at the map. "The Beauly River, Scotland, with a small island in it, called Eilean Aigas—Eagle Island."

Valerie bent forward to look, while, behind her, Dulcie had jumped on the couch and begun to sharpen her claws on the blanket thrown over it.

"Dulcie, stop that!" he said, and she did for a few moments, then continued." Ah, she's a real woman, she doesn't listen!" he added with a small laugh.

Turning from the map to face him, she asked, "Is that what you really think?"

"It must be if I said it. However…I have never been in a stable relationship like yours, Valerie."

"Nor are you ever likely to be with that sort of cynicism!"

They both halted. He remembered Adrian saying she had a frontier sense of justice.

"You may be right. Perhaps I'm too old a dog to learn new tricks," he added.

"I meant to express the opposite. Where there's life, there's hope."

"Thank you for taking an interest in my welfare. Come through, I have something else to show you." Out into the hallway again, then he opened a door into—a closet. There was a circular plate of metal on the wall, and he removed it to light up a screen, and pushed a button. A long shot of a city appeared, then slowly coalesced.

"Oh, my God, that's Houston!" she gasped.

"Yes, it is," he answered with a laugh." It's NASA, to be precise."

"What—"

"The Sidi thought I might enjoy being a 'watcher' for this NASA project—its GPS has been scattered around the world."

"Oh."

"Let me punch in some coordinates." Up popped Switzerland, narrowing down toward Basel.

"Amazing."

"It does keep me entertained."

"And—this picture beside it—?"

"It is a chap I admired, a prosecutor in Sicily, Giovanni Falcone. He was assassinated in 1992 by the Mafia."

"Are you afraid?"

"At times, of course." *No one else would have asked me that. They would either think they are being tactful, or don't want to listen.*

CHAPTER 4

Carter arrived at St. Stephens via private car.

He exited the car, turned his head slightly to the left, saw no one he knew, then turned his head to the right, and there he was: Adry, Adrian's son. The closer he came, the more certain some of Adry's features were so familiar to Carter, he was momentarily stunned. Same walk, same stature, some of the same facial looks.

He held out his hand and blurted, "You have filled out since last I saw you!" *What a stupid thing to say!*

"An advantage of living in London: a local gym. And you?"

"I still run every morning, although for the last three years, it has always been on a treadmill." Adry was escorting a young woman fresh as spring itself, in an underdress of light blue with a transparent material imprinted with flowers on top of it, wearing gloves.

"Would you introduce me to your young lady?"

"This is Brie Montagu, Carter, my fiancée."

"My goodness, is this recent?"

"Since yesterday," said Adry with a big smile.

"Does your mother know?"

"Of course. Brie, this is Sir Carter Braxton."

"Hello, Sir Carter."

"Just Judge will do, Brie."

"Oh, don't you like being called a Sir?"

"Not especially, particularly by people I know!"

As she extended her hand, he noticed she wore fingerless gloves. They entered the church to find Valerie, in a tweed suit and a hat, holding down a pew. She looked up to see Carter, and started; he was dressed in an elegant suit with a print silk necktie. *Where did that come from?*

When he sat down next to her, Valerie reviewed how to insert four fingers into the *Book of Common Prayer,* which he vaguely remembered from going to church with them at Pendragon. Beside him, three voices sang lustily, so when communion came, she stayed with him, and he did not protest as she thought he might. She noticed he did not seem focused on the service at all, but instead on some inward struggle. He seemed relieved when the service was over.

Adry had rushed out to grab a taxi. There was the same car waiting for Carter. "Valerie—would you mind riding with me?"

"I'll meet you there," she said to her son.

Once inside the car, he said, "I had the most—frightening experience in there. I felt the ceiling was going to collapse."

"Aha."

"What was it, Valerie?"

"The devil didn't like to see you in church."

"You mean the fellow with a pitchfork and horns?" *These last years surely have unsettled her mind.*

"Yes, that is what I mean and yes, I am still in my right mind."

"How did you know what I am thinking?"

"It's the usual question when I mention the subject."

"I wish we had the time for explanation."

"Have you ever read Lewis's *Screwtape Letters?* He's an Oxonian like yourself."

"No, I have not."

"I realize you will not have the same relationship with us as when Adrian was alive, Carter. I simply thought I'd see if aught of our friendship remained. There's no etiquette for a widow to measure former relationships, and if they still apply. I just blunder along."

Rules was just the same, which is how it ought to be, as London's oldest restaurant. Their table was in the back, with a banquette against the wall, while Carter and Valerie took chairs.

Gabrielle removed her gloves which disclosed a sparkling ring on her finger.

"Oh, lovely!" Exclaimed Valerie. "It certainly cleaned up nicely!" (For Brie had chosen to have Adry's grandmother's ring.)

"Excuse me." Carter got up to find a waiter and ordered a bottle of vintage champagne. (He had noticed in the past that sentimental occasions always mustered better service). Valerie noted the gesture, and concluded Carter had finished his training as a gentleman.

"Perhaps we should toast an engagement and a new enterprise," said Valerie.

"Why not." The four of them touched glasses.

"Yes, Adry added, "Now that Mum has revivified our finances a bit, and I am to marry a woman who sculpts in wood, we have a new line -up."

Carter noticed that Brie was somewhat conscious of her hands, which betrayed several scars from chiseling, and that her hands were stronger than one would suspect.

"I am glad to hear Pendragon will continue."

Their order came and conversation wilted. Yet after finishing the entrée and awaiting coffee and dessert, Carter said to Valerie, "Is Adry conversant with the subject I raised on our way here?"

"Why, yes!"

"What is it?" Her son asked.

"Your mother has presented me with the thought there is a specific cause for evil. I deal with evil every day, yet I must confess this is a new hypothesis to me."

"One that *we* believe," said Adry, firmly. *He certainly has his father's certitude.*

"I shall have to look into it," Carter said. "I have plenty of time available to think. What do you advise for reading?"

"*Screwtape Letters*. I'm afraid it's one we always suggest. It is the gentlest introduction to the subject."

"Adding metaphysical evil would certainly complicate an already complicated problem."

"You don't have to be a theologian, Carter. You are a judge. You only have to deliver secular justice."

"It's just as well. I not a religious man."

"Why not? Dad was," queried Adry."

"I think we had an unspoken agreement not to touch upon that subject," said Carter."

"Yes, Dad did not to hassle people about their disbelief. Why did you come to church with us?"

"To honor your father's belief, Adry. I am not so insensitive as not to realize his beliefs held great value for *him*."

By now they had finished and were standing on the pavement outside the restaurant. Adry began to flag down a cab, and Carter's safe automobile arrived.

"Valerie, shall you be able to drink tea with the Sidi?

"What time and where?"

"The Savoy, four o'clock."

"I'll meet you there."

Carter held out his hand. "Adry, I am delighted to see you again, as well as meet your intended." They shook hands.

From inside his car, he watched them pile into the taxi, chatting animatedly. He found he was disinclined to part, and feeling rather lonely. He asked the driver to pass by a bookstore and sent him inside to purchase a copy of *The Screwtape Letters*.

CHAPTER 5

Adry insisted on accompanying his mother to the Savoy, to check out what kind of encounter this would be. Carter was already there, and had checked his Burberry with *The Screwtape Letters* in the pocket. He was waiting in the lobby. Valerie gave her son a kiss, then she and Carter crossed the magnificently green carpeting which ran all over the ground floor, down three steps into to the tea room, which spread out all the way to the Thames at the back of the room. It took only a moment for Valerie to pick out one of the tallest men in the room, his back to the river so he could view the lobby. He stood up as they moved toward him.

The Sidi smiled approvingly at Carter. "Ah! Very nice," he remarked at Carter's outfit. Valerie did not know it, but the Sidi was an inveterate shopper. It was he who bought such elegant clothing for Carter.

"Mrs. Falconer," he said, bowing over her hand. "Such a pleasure to meet you. Are you bringing the young man I saw in the lobby with you?"

"That is my son Adry, on his way to walk his fiancée's dog."

Western style suit, neatly trimmed short beard, darker complexion, but not as dark as some of the other faces. Perhaps Oxbridge, perhaps Sandhurst, thought Valerie.

"One of my wives has showed me a sticker you designed on one of her grocery shopping expeditions. It was a gentleman wearing white tie evening wear with a Stetson hat and cowboy boots leading a steer with an 'H' brand. Very amusing!

"I hope she bought the roast beef!"

"Certainly. We are not thieves! The paint seems to have an unusual clarity."

"Yes, I use the old method of gesso. Pigment and egg yolk." Valerie noticed hotel staff roping off the entrance to the tea room, so no one could see into its corners.

The Sidi gestured toward them: "An unusual indulgence," he remarked.

Is this man seeking to impress me? The Sidi sat down with his back to the wall, so he could see in either direction. *Well, he has.*

"You have seen the manner in which we have safe housed Carter."

"I believe so."

"You understand it is not to be divulged to anyone?"

"Of course!"

"Some of my operatives are here with me. Would you like to take a guess who they are? I would like to make sure they are inscrutable."

"Not me! I haven't a clue," replied Valerie.

"Try. What about that small Chinese woman near the window?"

"Oh, she's too small."

Sidi smiled. "That woman has trained at least half of the personal guards of the sheikhs and kings of the Middle East in kung fu." He laughed. "One king gifted her with two white Arabian stallions. She does not ride. Yet to give them away would be an insult!"

"Why doesn't she put them out to stud? That would be a compliment and someone else would have to feed them!"

"I will make that suggestion, but, she does not work with us."

"Why?"

"Because we are men, of course. That is improper. What about you, Carter? What about that fellow over there?"

"He has an impression in his hair from the band you wear around your headpiece."

"Not bad. He is one of my drivers. A security person would never leave such a clue."

"I do recognize that chap over there."

"Yes, of course you know Khalil. I am afraid we must go upstairs to finish our discussion."

"Why?"

"It must be confidential."

Valerie and Carter took the freight elevator with the Sidi and Khalil up to the seventh floor, as Valerie experienced another aspect of security. When the door to their suite opened, Valerie noticed bedding rolled up in one corner.

"These beds are no good," said the Sidi. "All they are good for is to fall out of." He sat down in a wing chair.

"Now, Mrs. Falconer," he said, "Carter has raised the subject of tiring of his solitude. There is a possible solution, should he wish to utilize it."

"And that is—"

"…To move him somewhere and see if we can draw Norway out. We are pledged to protect him wherever he is."

Going down, they were able to leave by the guest elevator.

When Carter reclaimed his coat, Valerie noted the book peeking out of his pocket.

"Yes, Valerie," he replied, with a smile.

CHAPTER 6

After leaving Valerie at her hotel, Carter went back to his flat and, soothed by a good meal, he was back at Oxford in memory. He had none of that important thing, a social circle; he did not have the wardrobe, manners, or the accent to fit in. But he realized this could be remedied. He took voice lessons and worked in a bookstore to acquire enough money for a suitable wardrobe.

One day at the end of spring term he was jogging by the river when he spotted an eight-man racing shell missing one rower. Adrian called to him, "Could you take a seat?" Indeed he could. He stayed in Oxford that summer, working and learning to row, for he was already in good shape. Now he had a group, much to his amazement.

Then Adrian invited him to Pendragon. He read up on country attire and arrived looking as if he had come out of a movie set, and was surprised to find sheep mowing the lawn.

He had to admit his main interest in visiting was to spend time with Adrian. His parents were delightful but distant, giving Adrian room to entertain his guest.

It was here that he first met Adrian's fiancée Valerie, who arrived from America on a visit. Valerie was an unobjectionable backdrop then. She was somewhat withdrawn, trying very hard to accommodate to her new situation. Her family owned a ranch in Texas, a business which engendered a measure of solitude, somewhat like Adrian's home in the Forest of Dean. He was able to watch her gradually imbibe the manner of her new situation. While he watched her, he drank in the manners of the family himself.

It was a June wedding after Adrian graduated. Carter came with several other members of the rowing team, all slightly off-center because Adrian was marrying an American. He met Valerie's family in the reception line, and listened hard to their Texas accent just as he imagined they were struggling with his. Roulon was wearing a bespoke British double- breasted tuxedo he had ordered in England after World War 2. Buddy wore what he was told was a Texas tuxedo, while Charlie and George simply wore items made in the United States. Valerie's mother Mabel wore a formal dress. George was a widower, and was accompanied by two boys who appeared Oriental. The top-off was Charlie's wife Claudia, who was dressed at the height of fashion.

When the children were born, he had expected to become more peripheral, but that did not happen. Valerie was perfectly comfortable with people breezing in and out, as had been true at her own home in Texas. Adrian introduced him to reading the Arthurian legends to Adry and Stella, so when he came, Adry would immediately hide his brief so he could not find it, making him free to read to them.

There were four years when he only visited briefly, when he was married and then divorced from Norah.

When she returned to Pendragon after her visit to London, Valerie had an unexpected call from the Sidi. To help overcome Carter's complaint about solitude, he asked if she would adopt a discrete telephone line that only ran between their two numbers; no one could dial out or receive calls. To be even safer, they were not to discuss safehousing issues or anything connected with that during a phone call.

Valerie was eager to do so now, as there now was a solitude for her as well, with Adrian and his parents gone. All she had to talk to was the children, with Adry now in London. One phone was put in the bedroom, another with a paint- splattered table in her studio.

The first ring she picked up nervously.

"Hello?"

"Carter here, Valerie."

"What are you doing now in court?"

"It's a matricide, schizophrenic: son kills mother, who has taken him in."

"'Home is the place where you go, and they have to take you in,'" she quoted.

"Quite so. It's a Section 20. We shall have testimony as to whether the defendant was taking his medications regularly, witnesses as to the mother's state of mind, queries as to whether she complained to the police or mental health facilities—which should or should not have led to the removal of the son from the house." One verdict, he continued, was not guilty by reason of insanity.

"At first, Valerie, it leads some defendants assured they have avoided penalty, until they realize they have gotten into a situation with no term limit except by reason of whether or not the authorities consider them 'cured.'

"A great deal in sentencing is whether the defendant is capable of taking his medication regularly or not. After the trial, I shall have to sentence him, of course."

"Oh! Is there anyone to help you there?"

"I have the trial notes, as well as the summations from the C.P.S. – Crown Prosecution Service. And I have sentencing guidelines. As well, there is public interest to consider—a high intolerance of children who kill parents, especially the mother. Too light a sentence would cause a stir."

"I'm glad I'm not you."

"Of course, Valerie, no judge does that perfectly."

"Then you have to live with all your decisions?"

"Righto." *I hope that sounded casual enough.*

"I'll say a prayer for you."

"Thank you, Valerie. May I call to tell you the results?"

He had assumed that these tragedies had made her lose her faith, but although it must have been severely buffeted, it had obviously survived.

"Of course."

After this conversation, Carter had a mental picture of the several times he had seen Valerie wearing earphones. He had merely thought they were to block some noise, yet upon re-visiting this picture he realized that the business was far enough from the house to make no noise.

Another picture succeeded this one. During a one- year period, the Falconers had been working on a new staircase, which meant everyone used the back staircase, which no one seemed to mind. Carter had only been able to admire part of it due to being partially klkkcolor blind. First, new flooring was put down to receive the stairs; there was a debate even Carter noticed between using bleached wood, or wood that had been bleached white by soap stoning, imported from Scandinavia. Soap stone won out. There were many coats of varnish on it, the last having a substance mixed in it to make it slip proof. The stairway ran up two stories, from the ground floor to the second floor, narrowing at the first floor.

The rounded banister was painted in what he had been told was oxblood red; instead of all the spindles being circular, all were squared in shape and run through with iron rods; they supported vertical spindles which intersected with the horizontal ones, which gave it a rather unique look. That he could appreciate. Then the spindles were painted with gleaming red Japanese lacquer. As for the stairs, it had taken genius of color to match the spindles with rose colored carpeting for the treads, with tile for the risers. Adrian seemed to be inordinately proud of the finished product, especially the color usage. Who would that have been in the Falconer family—Valerie. All in wood, of course.

When he called the next time, Carter said, "Now, Valerie, it is your turn."

"To what?"

"Talk."

"I don't know where to start."

"Let me ask you a question, then."

"All right."

"I recall when I visited seeing you wear headphones. What were they for?"

"Oh. I was reading."

"Beg pardon?"

"I was listening to a book. I have a reading disability. I read very slowly."

Adopting his best barrister mode, he kept asking questions. "When did they find this out?"

"When my brother Charlie first met his wife, Claudia."

"I see."

"Charlie had gone to New York to talk to a lawyer about advertising. That's how he met Claudia."

"She is the lawyer?"

"Yes."

"Did you say they were married?"

"Yes, we have a Gulfstream."

"They commute?"

"Yes. Claudia was embarrassed to have this big galoot in western gear on her hands; he wanted to take her out for dinner so he asked where was a good place to eat, she answered, 'Jacob Worth.' Then he asked her where it was, she said, 'Boston.' She thought that would be an obvious brush off. But he said, 'I'll pick you up at 5.30. We have a Gulfstream.' He didn't even bother to ask where, he elicited her address from her secretary. She was the last hired—"

"…first fired," he said.

"That's right, so she persuaded herself she ought to go to see if she could land him, which would certainly enhance her career. While they were eating, he mentioned his little sister—me—who was doing so miserably in school; she asked if I ever had been tested for a reading disability, and if not, he should have it done immediately and call her with the results."

"Did he?"

"Indeed—he was smitten!"

"And you?"

"Carter—it was like becoming a whole different person. Heretofore, I was my mother's embarrassment. I think sometimes she thought I was faking it just to annoy her. And then—I wasn't. The year I was nineteen I came east to take art classes in Boston and stayed with my grandparents in Concord, who introduced me to talking books. I caught up on so many things!"

CHAPTER 7

Carter replaced the receiver slowly and thoughtfully. He realized he had just been speaking with another person who had to struggle her way up.

Carter always aspired to London ladies. They fulfilled his portrait of who he had become, yet with whom there was finally an unfulfilled distance. Whenever he felt tenacles tightening, he fled the relationship—he did not want another Norah, yet this conundrum had prevented him from settling down. In the lee of the breakup of such relationships, he had returned to sporadic dating.

While he was lost in such reflections for a day or two, Valerie received a letter from her father. It jarred her. He was full of admiration for whoever it was who had stopped interference of crude shipping in and out of the south coast, as they had tried everything, yet without success. He would love to meet her legend and congratulate him, as well as find out how he accomplished this.

Should she mention it to Carter. Why not. All they could say was no. She knew he had a fax machine in his home office: they had one at the business. She sent a letter from there, and rang him to tell him she had sent the letter.

Their next conversation was more in Valerie's court. Yes, he had read *Screwtape*. What did he think? He took the point yet felt the points were embroidered with a bit of precious prose.

"After all, it's not just an essay—he's a writer."

"Touché. I'd rather have your take on the devil."

"Let's start with what God asks Satan where he has been, and the latter replies, 'Roaming the earth and patrolling it.' Why? He is the Prince of this world. How did he get here? In Isaiah we read, "how hast thou fallen, bright morning star?" Jesus says "I saw him fall like lightening." He has been cast out of Heaven, traditionally, along with one third of all the angels; it is called the transcendental fall. He arrived in Eden before Adam and Eve as the tempter, and creates original sin, making humans capable of evil—first outworking out of Eden, brother kills brother."

"Why? Isn't this God-chap supposed to be omnipotent?"

"Theodicy is very complicated, but we do know from Job sometimes God grants the devil permission. Pope Leo Xlll is supposed to have heard such a dialogue between God and the devil."

"Who was the victim?"

"The church."

Carter gave a little whistle. *We are definitely shifting gears!* "So this can apply to something larger than a person?"

"Definitely. Winston Churchill wrote in his series on World War 1, in reading a bedside Bible when he was visiting in Scotland, he was assured England would win World War 1."

This is definitely the deep end of the pool! "And how, pray tell?"

"Deuteronomy chapter 9, first 5 verses. You can check it out."

"I don't, alas, possess a Bible."

"I'm sure your landlord could buy you one. And remember, mankind is quite capable of creating its own evil."

I thought she might offer to send me one. She is tougher than that. Not at all like my usual run of females.

"Speaking of my landlord, Valerie, he has the odd belief that anyone who truly wants to meet him, and is sincere and discreet, is a messenger."

"My father should come?"

"Is he sincere and discreet?"

"I think so. "

"The Sidi will want him to stay at his building. Not go to visit his family."

"I will tell him all that."

Valerie sat down after she rang off and wrote to her father, empathizing security.

Her father wrote back that he would arrive next week, with airline number flight, ETA, and carry-on luggage. As used as she was to his ability to make decisions quickly, she was still a trifle startled. She walked down to a business office and faxed his letter to Carter. Adry had started up a part of the facility and seeing the lights on and some simple machinery starting to run made her rejoice.

CHAPTER 8

As for Carter, he was a bit uneasy at this turn of events, for he had been part of everything prior, but this was to be just between the Sidi and Roulon Herrington. It was even stranger for Valerie to have a family member landing in England and being unable to greet or visit with them.

Roulon was informed that he would be met by a sign-bearer, not having 'Herrington' on the sign, but Jameson. After clearing customs, Roulon walked toward him, carrying an overnight bag in his left hand. He still limped slightly on his right leg, and used a cane in his right hand, for he had suffered a stroke two years before, and regained his walking only with intensive therapy.

The man who met him was English, not Arabic, and drove a car with darkened windows, which ended its journey in the underground garage. The driver carried his bag to the elevator. When Roulon exclaimed "A bit tight in here," the man replied, "I'm sorry, that is a part of our security," When they reached the fifth floor, the man explained to Roulon he would take the suitcase to his accommodation.

"Take me, too," said Roulon. "I'd like to clean up."

"The Sidi expects you would want to, and also, take a bit of a rest," replied the driver. "Would you care for something to eat?"

"Toast," said Roulon, staying on the safe side, not knowing what the 'something' might be.

The man spoke into the telephone: "One order of toast to the guest room. May I hang out your clothing, sir?"

"Is that what you are supposed to do?"

"Yes, sir."

"Then go ahead and do it. I'm going to take a shower." He noticed a pitcher beside the toilet, but had no idea it was part of Muslim cleansing practices.

Emerging from his shower, Roulon donned a white terry cloth robe he found hanging on the door. Not feeling like clothing himself again, he slipped on his pajamas, put the robe on, sat down on the bed, and heard a tap on the door. "Come through," he said, remembering that he was in England. It was his toast, with butter in a side dish. "Put her right there," he indicated, nodding to the bedside table. He put several pillows behind him and the bed board, and sat, munching, when there was another tap on the door. "Come," he said.

A man entered, wearing a long Arabic robe, then sat on a chair he pulled over next to the bed. "Good evening, Mr. Herrington, I am Sidi el-Hassem. I trust you have had a comfortable trip."

"Yes, indeed. Business class."

"I do not plan to start talking until tomorrow, when you have rested."

"Mighty obligin' of you."

In the morning, he rang for breakfast on what was strictly a house phone. After dressing, he rang the Sidi to alert him that he was ready with his questions. The Sidi came and invited him into his office. There was a large map of the world on the wall, with red lines from place to place.

"These are the pipelines we are watching," his host informed him.

"I see that ours are already gone. Tell me, Sidi, how do you finance all these operations?"

"Ah, a first American query! It is always money!"

"I'm sorry to be so predictable."

"It is a question which is bound to come to the surface sooner or later. I shall answer it and get it out of the way. It is self-financed. We have a financial base run by my eldest son, Rashid."

"He must be a whiz!"

"Yes, but also, he has help from a number of family members—I have twenty-five children."

By how many wives, I wonder?

"Why are you doing this?"

"Because it needs being done. 'Expend one's possessions for the good of others,' says our Koran. Some of this oil stealing can cause wars."

What can I say? He's absolutely right. "But, if you don't mind answering me, what is your motivation?"

"It would be what you Christians might call the outworking of caritas."

"I see. Then I take it you are a religious man."

"I am a practicing Muslim."

"How do you collect the information you must have?"

"I cannot say more than we have satellite tracking privileges."

"I don't think even a man of such wealth as yourself could build one."

"You are quite right. As it happens, we are safeguarding a judge who has been threatened by assassins who have been hired by one of the men this judge convicted and sentenced."

"British or American?"

"British."

A bell went off in Roulon's head. "I recall my daughter writing that her husband had a best friend who was a High Court judge—this wouldn't be the man, would it? She did say they hadn't heard for him for quite a while…"

"Yes, I believe I met your daughter recently— Mrs.Falconer.

"That's her."

There was a pause in the conversation as Roulon surveyed some framed photographs on the wall.

"You are looking at my photographs? I took them myself over a period of three years, when I was a young man."

"What is it?"

"Our Lady of Zeitoun. You must look closely to see her form. There was a definite spot on the roof that she preferred. The church is in Zeitoun, a suburb of Cairo, supposedly where Joseph and Mary fled after they had been warned by the wise men."

"'Our Lady' sounds Catholic."

"They are Coptic Catholics. They have their own Pope."

"To what end?"

"To what end? I will tell you my interpretation. She is beginning a mission I call the Children of Abraham."

"Oh." There was a silence. Roulon was thinking. Finally, he said, "There is no doubt all three religions began with Abraham. What do you believe is your involvement in this?"

The Sidi smiled, "Mr. Herrington, in the past, it was merely to apprise people of her existence. Now I am beginning to grow too old to actively participate in our current projects. I only do the planning. My cousin Khalil guides carrying them out. I believe that my role will change as I grow older."

Roulon was pleased the Sidi had shared his vision with him.

"I forgot to say that healings took place there, which I think were symbolic as well as physical. Already we have connections— for example, Judge Braxton has been mentored by a Jewish scholar, Nathan Levi."

"Reading between the lines of my daughter's letter, I gather there is some discontent in the Judge. Where is he living?"

"On the top floor of this building with an upward escape to a helicopter. He is starting to feel he is no longer part of the human race. We have been discussing alternatives. Perhaps we shall decide to move him to draw his assassins out. We are surveying possible locations."

"I've got one you might consider," said Roulon.

The Sidi looked surprised. "That is kind of you, but don't you need to consider it further?"

"No, I'm the boss at my place. We have a house formerly occupied by one of our foremen that is far away from the main house, and from which you can see clearly in all directions."

"I would want to also consult the local police."

"The local police wouldn't handle something like this. You'd have to talk to the Texas Rangers. They are involved in Intelligence."

"You are well informed."

"I know my way around my own backyard. By the way, if these guys will start tracking him, how do you plan to get him out of the country without a passport?"

"I plan to board him on an RAF military transport at Brize Norton. Eventually this would draw our man out to try to find him." The Sidi looked pleased by Roulon's question.

"May I go to look at this place myself?" the Sidi asked him.

"Hell, yes!"

CHAPTER 9

"Cowgirl on board, cowgirl on board! K4 READY FOR TAKEOFF!"

Valerie had been driven to Brize Norton, while another woman had been sent to imitate her as 'she' left from Pendragon for an hour's drive to a shopping mall. She would shop for another hour, then drive an hour back to Pendragon. By this time, Valerie was at the RAF's facility for transport and freight aircraft, not the sexy fighters berthed on Anglesey.

She had been driven to the shipping building where she was cleverly hidden beneath some light luggage which was taken on board the Tristar.

Carter, Khalil and Mohammed had preceded her into the passenger area of the plane, which was built to accommodate 130 passengers; the empty seats gave it a sepulchral aura. She and Carter sat a few rows apart from each other.

The captain came to the cockpit door. "We are lightly loaded and have an extra tank of fuel. To explain, we will practice fueling a fighter plane *en route.*"

The engines started maneuvering the Tristar onto the nine-thousand-foot runway. It stuck to the ground a bit longer than a commercial jet, but finally they were airborne.

Valerie had begged a ride on the expedition. "I haven't had the wherewithal to visit my family in several years," she pleaded.

As for Carter, he was a bit shaken to leave his safe haven of three years, and felt like an inmate coming out of prison. His mind was still unsettled by the speed at which things had happened; the Sidi had looked at the Texas possibility, taken photos and videoed it, showed it to Carter, talked to Roulon (including the possibility of air conditioning) and told Carter that among the team he would send with him were his two best men, Khalil and Mohammed, who was also a doctor. Then photographs and maps had appeared, the latter with marked elevation lines, which Khalil followed as if it were an easy book, while he pointed out various geographical features. Carter tried to follow their deliberations but had to admit they were beyond him after a certain point, and began to get a headache. The Sidi told him to sit down and relax.

When a man serving as steward asked if he would like a Scotch, Carter was glad to have Haig & Haig to quell a bit of his unease, although he would have preferred a single malt. He hoped Valerie would sit with him so he would have someone to talk to, but she took a sleeping pill and stretched out across three seats. Her pocketbook fell over and spilled some of its contents on the floor. He was able to note that she had a dual passport. So, she had never become a fully British citizen.

An hour had passed when the cockpit door opened again. "We're deviating slightly from our course now in order to top off this fighter plane. Look to your left side." Carter moved to the left side to look out the window. Soon, a small speck appeared on the horizon, speeding toward them so quickly its size grew by leaps and bounds, somewhat like a baby elephant nearing its mother to nurse. *This is coming much too fast!*

It was coming straight at them. He heard the noise of a fuel line beginning to unroll from the Tristar, and suddenly he felt the same terror that he had at St. Stephens.

We're going to crash.
I am going to die.
What will happen to me when I die?

Thoughts dizzied his mind. He had always been of the school of thought "Just throw me in a hole in the ground" when he died.

Then, his mind was so overcome by the fear he could hardly think.

He fainted, arms gripping the arms of the chair, eyes closing.

He did not see the jet suddenly turn sideways and match its speed to theirs, then fuel flow from the Tristar into its tank, see the pilot wave to their pilots, then pull away, as the hose wound up. When he woke, it was with a start; as he opened his eyes, he did so warily, wondering where he was. He was soaked in sweat and hoped he had not accidently urinated.

What had happened…

There was some power which was not at all interested in his sophisticated thought patterns, his role as a High Court judge, even his predicament. All that mattered was his essence, which, he had to admit, was a bit pretentious. Whatever it was did not subscribe to ritual at all, the kind to which he was daily acquainted; the all rise, the prosecutor and defense, and—he had to admit—the fear on the faces of those involved in the trial—with which he could not professionally empathize.

He had been taken to church by his mother in his humble childhood, on occasion when his father would let them go. And— looking at it honestly—he had absorbed more of his father's attitude than his mother's—yes, that man from whom he thought he was so different. Was that lack of attendance in the church somehow influenced by him? The thought shocked him, because he knew it was true.

When would that woman wake up so he could talk to her?

It would not be too soon, he realized.

The Tri Star rumbled along at less than the speed of a commercial liner. A book tucked in his carry on to read called to him, but he could only read sporadically; a miasma of thoughts soon began pounding through his head, which forced him to stop to let them carry him away. Dark turned to light as they flew west, with time changing as the earth turned. Finally they landed at Andrews Air Force base to refuel.

Valerie began to stir. As they braked to a stop, the door opened, and Mohammed walked back to encourage him to walk and to get down to breathe some fresh air. "Let me check your pulse," the doctor added.

"Why?"

"You fainted, honorable judge. Your pulse was somewhat elevated when I last checked it." Philosophically Carter held out his wrist. Mohammed's fingers gripped it.

"Ah, yes, back to normal. There is no infibulation."

Walking about, Carter breathed in fresh air deeply. Valerie appeared. She seemed to be looking about for something, and she found him; a Spanish- looking man she ran over to and cried, "Hello, Diego!"

"Carter!" she called. "Kahlil! This way!"

They followed her until Carter got the surprise of his life: Diego was the pilot of a private Gulfstream, obviously owned by the Herrington family. But Valerie pointed out that the family wealth was not liquid, but tied up in equipment, manpower, cattle, oil, taxes—et cetera. "The Gulfstream is a business expense," she pointed out. "At first we just rented one."

He wanted to talk to her. He figured the best way to achieve it was bluntness. So as the four of them returned to the aircraft, he said to Valerie, "I would like to talk to you. That fear overcame me again this time." She sat down by the window, and he sat on the inside.

Hearing of his experience, Valerie sat thinking. "I'd credit the devil with your experience with us in church," she said, "but this—it was very powerful and I just don't know."

"Can I tell you of an experience I had in 1992?"

"Of course."

"Italian television was given permission to capture the funeral of the chap in the picture on my wall-Giovanni Falcone. I was still in my own flat at the time, thus I was able to watch it. First it panned around the church, which was so ornate it made this poor boy's eyes pop. There were pillars, arches, decorations, confessionals, chandeliers, decorative carving, paintings statues, with strategic gold lines. The camera moved up front where there were seven coffins arranged in a semi-circle. The bodyguards' caskets were draped in red, and Giovanni and his wife Francesca's coffins had their black judges' robes flung over them, the announcer explained, communicated in subtitles. Behind them I could hear the noise that accompanies people shifting in their seats, sneezing, coughing, squirmy children, and women searching for things in their pocket books. The service began, and things grew quieter; but at some point, there was a dead silence.

"The only sound was the footsteps of a young woman, the widow of one of Falcone's bodyguards. All that had been left of him was one hand. Her name was Rosario Schifoni, and she mounted the steps for the pulpit.

"In the name—" she began, then shifted, "though first, I ask for justice," she began. "Then this remarkable woman went on to speak to the Mafia, for, as she said, because I know even inside this church there are Mafiosi, and that even they had a chance for forgiveness. If you have the courage to change…be Christian. For this we pray in the name of the Lord who said on the cross, 'Father, forgive them for they know not what they do.'"

"I was told, not only did she not speak formal Italian, but in a very difficult Sicilian dialect. Imagine that, I thought to myself. And then, remarkably, the camera fixed on a crucifix, and somehow the Christ had a compassionate look on his face—or that was what I imagined. I was a judge, Valerie, and I had judged him the way I had imagined he would judge me, for I am a sinful man, I know full well."

"The devil always writes backward," she replied "He can really use the weight of sin to make you hate yourself rather than to be forgiven."

"I'm glad you can see it that way. I consider myself a hopeless case."

"Oh, no! I'll grant you've been a bit of a variety man, but you still have free will."

"Not for the last three years," he answered.

"Maybe you should get baptized."

"Why, for heaven' sake?"

"Thou hast said it—for Heaven's sake. For help not falling back into the same old rut."

"What do you think Adrian would have thought?"

"He'd be damn glad!"

"Did the two of you—ever talk about me?"

"How could we not have after all those years?"

"And what did Adrian think?"

"He never was a proselytizer, but he would have been happy if some of us rubbed off on you. He would have been happy if he'd been able to marry you off."

"I see."

There had been so many time changes in this journey, his sense of time was getting juggled, and now he was beginning to notice the landscape. Valerie asked Diego to circle Palo Duro Canyon. Diego made a sharp bank at enough of an angle that everyone seemed to tolerate but Carter, who suddenly said he feared he was going to throw up.

"Flatten out, Diego," Valerie called. "Diego was too close to forty-five degrees," she told Carter, "that's where people get sick if they are not habituated."

"I saw something that looked like a skeleton wind mill," he told her as they began to descend.

"We are over the Ogalla Aquifer between the Pecos and the Rio Grande; it's one of the biggest, and it pumps water up from underground."

Shortly thereafter, Diego brought them down on an unpaved runway behind the Herrington ranch house, from which it was separated by a mound. Over the mound, the house stretched out to the left, and a stable with an apartment above it to their right. A big man came running toward them, picked up Valerie and swung her around, howdying his little sis. Valerie introduced him to her companions. It was her brother Buddy. It was so hot, Carter didn't know if he was in hell or Texas.

"Come on, gents," he said, "I'm putting you in the apartment tonight—we have a window of time before this guy from Norway finds us!" Inside was a kitchen, large sitting room and four bedrooms. Apparently, Valerie had not seen it, because she was telling her brother how nice it was. Then she told Carter good night, and hurried over to the main house. After greeting members of the family who were still up, Valerie went to bed, and woke up sometime the next day dazed by jet lag. After showering and dressing, she went downstairs to find something to eat.

As she was drinking her coffee, her father came in and kissed the top of her head. "Mornin,' daughter," he said. "Are you with us yet?"

"Not quite, Pop."

"The Sidi fellow is going to come in a day or two, when we move the judge out to the foreman's house."

"He really seems to get around."

"He seems to stay on top of things."

"That, too."

"How are the rest of the family taking to him being here?"

"They've all been briefed. It'll be out of sight. We have a few days' time for them to meet him, before we move him."

"You aren't worried about our family?"

The Sidi had told them that they were not terrorists, they only shot who they came for.

The weather was cooler, with a breeze, and Valerie's father told her he had seen Carter wandering around outside. "Poor guy must think he's on the backside of the moon," he remarked.

"I'll go out and see," said Valerie, finishing her coffee.

"This isn't worrying you too much?" her father asked her.

"I'm not awake enough to worry!" She replied. She found Carter as her father had described him, wandering around, trying to make sense in his new surroundings. She wished him good morning.

"There are some chairs underneath those trees, are there not? Would you care to sit down?"

Once they were seated, he asked, "What did Adrian make of your ranch?"

Valerie laughed. "He was quite excited on his first visit to the so-called 'Wild West.' He remembered everything he had seen in movies. Of course, we no longer had any gunfights or open cattle drives or local saloons. Ranching isn't romantic, it's hard work. We've tried to diversify in case of famine or drought. I saw my first famine when I was eight years old and I still dream about it. Cattle died with their heads in the feed trough. I was a little girl and I cried. I probably still would. Once he asked one of our hands what cattle do. The guy said, 'Well, they jes' eat'n shit.'" She laughed heartily.

"I had the oddest dream last night."

"Do tell."

"I was walking down to the Coroner's Court to look over a corpse which pertained to the case I was trying. When the mortician pulled it out, it opened its eyes and looked at me."

"Shall these bones live?" Valerie commented.

"Let's hope so. I find my idea of time has become somewhat foreshortened."

CHAPTER 10

"Shall I walk you around?" she asked.

"That would be most agreeable."

They went in the front door, cut across several rooms, and entered her brother Buddy's office. There was a huge map on one wall; the ranch was not one whole parcel of land but separate pieces with red elevation lines and blue lines for rivers, streams and ponds, with sites of aquafiers numbered with the water depth of each underground supply marked with brown lines.

"We've got a continuous system with pipes to carry over spots the water doesn't reach," explained her brother. "These are locks. If one section is too low on water, I raise the locks to bring other water through. They all are on surveillance cameras, and this ticker keeps track of market prices. The boys take care of salt licks."

Carter felt a sense of disassociation confronted with something about which he knew nothing at all. He noticed a framed document of PhD. from Texas A. and M. on one wall with Buddy's name on it.

Going on, following Valerie, he arrived in a large kitchen with a cook at work. "If you want anything to eat you haven't got, ask Grace," Valerie said, and introduced him. Carter had visited occasional country houses, and being introduced to the cook was definitely not part of the protocol.

"What are these?" he asked, seeing a sort of white mush in a pot.

"Them is grits, Judge," Grace answered him

"It is usually associated with breakfast," Valerie told him. "but people also like to eat them plain with red gravy."

So his introductory course included new food. Somehow, he had not figured this in. However, he had done a bit of traveling, and he was not completely taken aback. In fact, he had developed a sense of curiosity about foreign foods which many English people did not.

He remembered Adrian's spiel once, in France, about British food. "Take a McDonald's hamburger," his friend had said. "First, we take the mayo off the bun, then we take the sesame seeds off it, get rid of the lettuce and tomato, and presto—it is ready to eat!" Memories of Adrian still floated across his brain, and he was sure it was more so for Valerie.

In late afternoon, out of the corner of his eye, Carter spotted Roulon on a brown horse, ride over to the corral, dismount, and hand the reins to one of the hands. He admired the utility of his gear: a coiled rope at one side of the saddle horn, a canteen on the other, a rolled up waterproof material of some sort behind the saddle and a rifle in a case slung at knee level. Walking toward the house, he muttered, "Afternoon, Judge," to Carter and promptly went inside.

Carter knew that a cocktail hour was planned for six o'clock, before dinner, in the stone room—the earliest room built on the property, with nice, thick walls, which made it cooler. Valerie had showed it to him; it was certainly built to repel invaders. Like the rooms he had seen in magazines, there were leather chairs, colorful blankets thrown here and there, while in one corner was a glass-door case, holding a collection of rifles that went back, as far as he could discern, for generations.

Valerie came down in a dress, and Roulon, in what Carter identified, from seeing them on Valerie, a clean pair of Levis and a cotton plaid shirt. He was gratified when Roulon introduced him all around, calling Carter with the title 'Judge.' Carter had brought several pairs of cotton trousers and he donned one of them with a polo shirt. To his surprise, he found that Khalil and Mohammed were also invited. He already knew Buddy and his wife Karen from the long-ago wedding, and now met their son, BJ. Charlie and Claudia were an unusual couple; Charlie tall, lanky, and tan, Claudia, petit and dressed at the height of fashion, without a tan. Karen took Carter by the elbow to guide him toward and elderly lady, sitting on a sofa—Valerie's mother—wearing a unique strand of real pearls in this situation.

"Don't be surprised at what she says, it just comes to her mind and out with it," Karen instructed. "Ma, this is Judge Braxton."

"Hello, young man."

"Charmed to meet you." *So this is the one who terrified Valerie.*

"What's that funny accent? The other one had it too. Why doesn't everyone talk the same. Wouldn't it be easier?"

"I believe it has been tried, Madame, but unsuccessfully." Somehow, the Tower of Babel came to mind from an infrequent Sunday school class.

"I'm glad we agree, young man." Karen stepped in and began to talk to her; Carter swung around to find Buddy approaching with glasses and some kind of whisky, with a young woman at his side. Carter, stunned, suddenly realized that Buddy had a daughter who, in English parlance, was a stunner. *Good thing I've had a steady practice of keeping a straight face!*

"Have some real whisky," said Buddy. "Old Forester bourbon." To his right, the cook was serving Khalil and Mohammed tall glasses of iced tea. He noticed a tall, balding blond man talking with them. Valerie joined them, and she motioned to include him. The blond balding man was talking about a book he had just read on Islam and its refined cleansing techniques.

"Why, your folk used toothbrushes all the way back in the seventh century!" The blond man was saying.

"No wonder they call our time period back then the Dark Ages!" volunteered Valerie.

Jack turned toward Carter and introduced himself.

"Jack is the pastor of our Living Waters Chapel," added Valerie.

"One of Roulon's pet charities," said Jack with a smile, who then repaired his interrupted conversation with Khalil and Mohammed, which appeared to surprise them. They had felt Jack was merely conversing with them until someone more of his ilk came along.

Here's someone to talk to." Over the years, Carter had developed a keen sense of which people were reliable and which were not.

"Have I met everyone in your family now?" Carter asked Valerie.

"No, my brother George lives in New York City and rarely has been home since he returned from VietNam. He only votes by telephone on our Directors' meetings."

"Oh?"

"It was he who urged us to use my little drawings and he was right."

"He is the brains of the family?"

"You might say so."

"Doesn't that bother your father?"

"You might say so. I think Dad visited him a time or two in New York."

Now Mabel wanted to know where Carter's wife was. "Shouldn't you have one?" She asked.

"Ma'am, I am not married."

"Were you ever?"

"Yes. I was."

"Pity. Have you met my daughter?"

"Yes, Ma'am, and I met you briefly at her wedding some time ago."

"I don't remember you."

"I don't expect that you would."

"What do you do?" *That old American question.*

Karen stepped in. "Mother, he is a High Court judge in England."

"You don't say."

Valerie was close enough to hear this last exchange and saw his expression change. *He tries to be humble, but he doesn't usually succeed!*

"Oh, England. What's the difference between it and America?"

"Adrian always said that if you had a waiter in England, he would remain a waiter, while one in America might develop into a millionaire. It's our class system," he explained.

"Oh?" Mabel was beginning to lose track of the conversation.

"However, you are an exception," replied Valerie, "considering where you came from!"

Yes, Clapham certainly does imply you have risen.

"What about that fellow who was your mentor?" asked Valerie.

"Nate? Yes. Ah. I owe him! He and Deborah have been my salvation."

"That's a strong statement."

"Yes, I was Nate's student, and I always thought he gave me very hard assignments because he thought there might be things a man of my background would not know. But then, some students illumined me that he only did that to students he felt were promising. On my tutorial I would stay up all night trying to come up with something he would not know—but I never succeeded. I was astonished one night when he invited me to dinner at his house. I still have dinner every Wednesday night with the two of them."

"His wife is—"

"Deborah. *How interesting it is that the only times I get talking to her, we go so deep.*

"They are practicing Jews?" asked Karen.

"Very much so. Nate says this three -year sequestration has been the best thing that has ever happened to me!" He actually laughed. It had been a while since that had happened!

"Interesting."

Indeed. I must be careful not to extend any anxiety from myself to her. She is already anxious enough, I'll wager.

He was right. She already had flashes of regret at being part of what had caused this situation for her family. Carter left her abruptly, returning to Jack. "Might I make an appointment with you?" asked.

"Appointment? You don't really need one. Why don't we find a place to talk?"

"One moment." Carter approached Khalil and asked if he might use their apartment. Silently, Khalil handed him the key. Carter returned to Jack, and showed him the key. Jack nodded; Carter did not wish to tell Valerie. He left the room and soon enough, Jack followed him.

Once in the common room of the apartment, Jack loosened his necktie. "Shoot."

"I have had some unusual experiences lately."

"Apart from being tracked by assassins?"

"Yes." Carter proceeded to tell Jack about his church experience and his airplane experience. "Someone suggested to me it might be a good idea to be baptized."

"Would that someone be Valerie?"

"Indeed."

"You are holding her at arm's length on this?"

"I would like to spare her as much of my anxiety as I can."

Jack laughed. "You know, Buddy always says his sister would charge into hell with an ice bucket."

Carter was silent.

"You also don't feel you want her to think she is bossing you around?"

"Probably."

"If the situation were reversed and she the person who was in trouble, wouldn't you want her to lean on you?"

"You think I pretend not to hear from her because she is a woman?"

"Highly possible. Anyhow, you have decided to be baptized. We could do it this Sunday. You're an adult. How much do you understand about it?"

"I am Mercy's godfather—I said the ritual for her."

"Baptism is intended to wash away the stamp of original sin."

"Does it?"

"Carter, if I didn't believe it was so, I wouldn't be in this line of work."

"How long does it last?"

Jack laughed. "Let's just say it gives you a clean start, which, at your age, could remove a lot."

"Yes, that's true," said Carter thoughtfully.

"Let's put it this way. Paul puts it that we put on our spiritual component after our natural self's tent has collapsed, we are reclothed in our rightful minds. That's why water is used. The transaction is that if we died with Christ, we will be raised with Christ—implying justification."

"I see."

"No, you really don't, this side of it."

"What activates this change?"

"The Holy Spirit. The same is true of the Catholic eucharist."

"You seem to be all over the place!"

"That's what nondenominational means."

"What will I have to do?"

"Baptism is usually a public sacrament, as the congregation participates with you. They are your spiritual helpers."

"This—would be the case on Sunday?"

"Unless you have sincere objections."

"Can I read something more about it?"

"Of course. What kind of pastor do you think I am? Let's ride out and I will get you one of my clever pamphlets."

It was thus Carter became acquainted with the Chapel of the Living Waters. Jack and he simply talked on the way out, which took about twenty minutes at a good speed. It was a simple wooden building made of beautiful oak, with pews instead of the chairs Carter was used to in European churches.

CHAPTER 11

Sunday morning dawned bright and clear. Before getting dressed, Carter lay on the couch in the common room. He was watching clouds as big as dreadnaughts float by. The sky seemed as big as eternity. Far off were the mountains.

Gone from mind were any comparisons with England's gardens. This landscape was like a whole new school of painting. He had packed a light grey suit, and, he discovered, a necktie Adrian and Valerie had assured him would match his suit. He didn't even remember packing it.

He gulped breakfast and went outdoors, standing still, taking in one thing after another. Generally, he did not notice his surroundings as he was too involved in thought. Yet this morning, he listened to the hoofbeats of the horses in the corral, the birds, (which he conceded had a right to live) cactuses, and the huge swathe of land before him. While he would never become a tree hugger, he did begin to notice the subtlety of leaves.

Valerie appeared, once again in a dress, and noticed the tie. "How nice of you to bring him along!" She remarked cheerfully.

"To bad it's too late."

"Better late than never."

Khalil was driving their rental car while Carter took the back seat with Mohammed, who was to the opposite side of the driver. *Protected from two sides,* he thought. The station wagons pulled up to the chapel—the Herringtons usually arrived at least a quarter of an hour early. Jack told Khalil and Mohammed he thought one of them in the lobby and one in the Choir loft upstairs would cover the pews, and that they did not have to obey the sign which read PLEASE CHECK YOUR FIREARMS.

"God will protect us," he said with a smile, "but He expects us to cooperate with Him!" Jack explained to Carter that in the right part of the service, he would just ask him to come forward to the baptismal font. "If you requested full immersion, we'd have to go down to the lake."

Little by little the congregation appeared. Some were ranch hands, some had long hair and beards, families trailing small children behind them, elderly women with knotted knuckles, some people with dark skin and straight black hair, who he learned were to be called Native Americans.

"How are you?" Valerie met him in the lobby.

"Rather uncertain as to who funds all this—your father??"

"It's a great tax write-off."

The Herringtons, he noticed, deployed themselves around the pews instead of sticking in a clump.

The service went smoothly, with Jack repeating some of it in Spanish. Then he called Carter forward. He announced that Carter wished to be baptized. Immediately, the congregation started clapping and cheering. *All that noise in a CHURCH?*

Carter stood by the baptismal fount, answering the ritual which was almost the same as the one he had said when Mercy was baptized. "Do you renounce the devil and all his works?" *That pesky fellow again.* He bent over and Jack poured a handful of water three times on his head, one for the Father, one for the Son, and one for the Holy Ghost.

Outside, tables and benches had sprung up; a grill was foaming delicious odors through the air. Hot dogs and hamburgers, sandwiches and urns of coffee, bottles of water were available. Several women were modestly breast feeding their hungry babies, changing rancid diapers. *All I am used to is nannies and prams rolling through the parks.*

Everyone came to congratulate Carter with whatever form of English they could muster, with many handshakes, slaps on the back, pats on the shoulder. Word went around that Carter was going to eat his first hot dog. This provoked a storm of advice about which condiment to put on it. He decided to try it plain.

Jack introduced Khalil and Mohammed to the congregation, who most people seemed at first to view as a miraculous visitation who had been far closer to where Jesus lived than they ever would be. They were besieged with questions. Had they ever been to Jerusalem? Khalil didn't mention that he had been there to meet with the Mossad. He drew simple pictures of the Dome of the Rock, the Wailing Wall, the Via Dolorosa. They were disappointed to find that the Jordan was narrow and muddy. It was standing room only at their table.

Valerie was going from table to table, glad-handing as she went. She bumped into Carter, who said, "—I took your advice, Valerie."

"Good. Now Mercy has a real godfather."

He sat down on a bench next to Roulon, "Good morning, Mr. Herrington."

"Call me Roulon, son."

"Good morning, Roulon."

"I see you are keeping an eye on my daughter."

"Both eyes, Roulon."

"Yup."

"I can see from her progress she knows how to work a room."

"Oh, yeah, I dragged her to all sort of local events."

"And your wife?"

"Mabel is beginning to drift," Roulon answered sadly.

When they returned to the ranch and Khalil checked in with the Sidi, he found that two of Norway's plants had gone to London to ascertain whether Carter had been moved from the fortress. When they discovered that he was also absented from court, it only confirmed their suspicions, and they also deduced that it was the Sidi who had arranged it. They had a big score to settle with him.

Buddy came to them and said, "I've got something to show you."

They went over the mound, and there was a Texas Ranger helicopter, with Buddy's friend Bobby Pearson leaning against it.

CHAPTER 12

Norway and his two operatives were temporarily stumped. Their leader decided the only real lead they had was that Valerie had been seen with Carter in England, so he deployed his troops there: one was to look over the telephone records of calls to and from Pendragon, another to search the Public Records Office for marriage licenses under Falconer, which would reveal Valerie's maiden name.

Norway was correct that the telephone books would be the more informative. Now they also had the name Herrington. The phone records demonstrated calls to two Herringtons in New York City, George and Claudia, and calls to a Wellspring in northern Texas.

First, they decided to observe New York. Checking in on the specifics of Claudia's and George's apartments, it was apparent they were not big enough to house Carter, the Sidi, and his men, let alone lend them protection. Their next stop was to book themselves on a flight to Abilene, Texas. The three men had stayed a few days in New York extra, to recover from jet lag.

"Here they come," announced the Sidi. He notified the police and the Texas Rangers, both of whom he had talked to before. The plan was to use unmarked cars around the perimeter where they were housed, as well as patrol cars at Wellspring. Rental businesses were asked to submit of reports on any and all passengers into Abilene who rented a car, along its license plates and VIN numbers.

At the foreman's unoccupied house, defenses began to ramp up. Buckets of sand and water, a foam jet container and gasmasks were brought in. Carter began to observe Khalil's energy grow; his mind, body, emotions were like shifting gears on a race car.

"What is all this for?" he asked his friend.

"The Sidi has studied their tactics in Nigeria, where it has worked very well. Their first move is to try to run their adversaries out of whatever shelter they are inhabiting, and they are able to launch incendiary or gas shells—or both. We are quite sure the incendiary will hit the highest part of the roof, so we have positioned all our fire equipment under the peak. As for gas, it is near the front of the house, so we can grab the masks very quickly. Also, the first thing they will do is cut the telephone lines, so we will communicate with Wellspring and the Rangers by two -way radio. The local police will be used to circle the perimeter. They are not trained to handle something like this. We would not wish to try to insert them in the mix. The Rangers will have a chopper on stand-by, and we can signal when and if we need something by two-way radio.

"You see, Carter, if we make no reaction, the Sidi is counting on curiosity about who may still be alive in the house driving them toward us. He would prefer not to have a gun battle."

Jack Tottle had appeared and demanded that they allow him to bind all the rooms before the action commenced. He had a bottle of holy water, and sprinkled it after he had said blessings at each corner. Being more familiar with strict lines between different branches of Christianity, Carter asked, "How did you get that, Jack?"

"At the local dispensary."

"Do they know that you did that?"

"What do you think the phrase nondenominal means?"

"Honorable judge, I think I have covered everything, but if you want to know something else, please ask me."

"What about machine guns or other automatic weapons?"

"These men are professionals, Carter. With automatic weaponry you cannot tell exactly where your target is. We can use rapid rifle fire, of course. But there is one such weapon in the sideboard in the dining room should we require it."

Carter sat listening these preparations seriously. He had to think of techniques to keep himself calm. The Lord Chief Justice's speech could not hold his attention, so he decided to try the Gospels.

The two- way radio began to crackle. The Rangers were in touch with the local police who were patrolling the perimeter. There was nothing to report yet. The Sidi and Khalil began to play an Arabic game which used dice, speaking in Arabic. Usually this did not bother Carter, but at this moment, he wanted to understand everything that was going on, and although he knew some Arabic expressions, he was too slow to follow this conversation. To his astonishment, he suddenly became very hungry.

He walked into the kitchen and looked into the refrigerator.

"Do not consume a heavy meal!" called Khalil.

Now the reason why the catering truck had appeared in these unlikely circumstances arrived: Carter found packets of familiar English sandwiches, as well as packets of hummus and other Arabic staples which he had never tried before.

Suddenly the choices became incredibly complex. Something new, or something tried and true? His nerves were so strained, the choice was almost superstitious—as if he ate the wrong item first, it would be a matter of life or death. He ate one of each, realizing that such monumental attention to a detail meant that his anxiety was moving toward panic.

Now the radio crackled. It was their Ranger base, who reported that the police just found an abandoned van, and wanted to know if they should impound it.

"Negative," said the Sidi, "It may be a backup, and I would assume they are in communication with their advance; the backup had best still be there."

"Wouldn't it be better if a Ranger were stationed there to receive progress reports?

"Only if he speaks Norwegian," said the Sidi.

After waiting several hours, at last the first assault came. It was an incendiary shell, and arced high, rather than coming in low.

Immediately Sidi's men ran up to the top of the stairwell to the second story, and waited there for the explosion, otherwise they would have been hit with flaming pieces or their clothing might have caught fire, or the concussion would have pushed them back against the walls—if, indeed, the walls held. The roof was already beginning to burn, shedding flame and smoke into the room. Two men took up extinguishers and concentrated on the roof; the other two started putting out flames that fell through to the floor. There was coughing caused by the smoke, and one man ducked out of the room to the top of the stairway to draw in enough breath to soothe his lungs. The Sidi and Khalil remained downstairs at the front windows, to see if the shell might be followed by Norway's men, but nothing moved toward them.

The noise, the flames, and the smoke terrified Carter so much, he disappeared back into the kitchen, where Mohammed had been sequestered in what was thought to be the safest room in the house.

"Do you want a sedative?" Mohammed asked.

"I've got my own." Carter opened a kitchen cabinet where he had stowed a bottle of Scotch. He began to sip it judiciously—*don't get a buzz on, just take the edge off.*

Then, everyone but the two sentries at the front windows filed into the kitchen. Now it was imperative to stay out of range of the windows, so Norway would not know whether they were inoperative or not. Bearing two large plates from the refrigerator, the men in the kitchen settled, cross legged, on the floor, with the plates in the middle of the circle. Carter took a chair.

Mohammed began to treat the upstairs men for burns; they did not flinch, although there were burn marks on their flesh, and holes in their clothing. They had stopped in the bathroom to wash the soot off their faces.

What would you like, honorable judge?" Khalil asked.

"Egg salad." Khalil lifted it up to him in the chair.

"Are you all right?" he asked solicitously.

"Almost." Carter was pale and still trembled slightly.

"Let them wonder if they have killed us with smoke, instead of driving us out of the house,"

Things went quiet, with Norway wondering why he had not driven them out of the house, but unsure of the real results. He sent one of his men, who moved from cover to cover. It was very hard, given the flat landscape, to get to the house; although the man tried to get close enough to see what had happened, he saw nothing.

Khalil raised his rifle. The Sidi put his hand on the barrel. "Don't shoot," he commanded.

"The advantage more often lies with the defenders," said the Sidi. *Sandhurst,* thought Carter. "The fact that the house is not still burning should tell them some of us are left. We should attach our gas masks." Khalil consequently went to the pile of impedimenta, handing the masks out.

"The wind is in their favor." This meant Norway could open a gas canister and let the lethal cloud drift toward the house.

They slipped into gas masks—with Khalil helping Carter— and crawled to the windows to stay out of sight. For Carter, it was menacing to watch the gas cloud drift silently their way. Carter heard his inhalations and exhalations inside the mask, while the oxygen was rather thin; the eyeholes were a bit dim and the whole mask claustrophobic. However, he stopped himself from retiring back into the kitchen. The cloud was now between them and Norway, so it was safe to peak out the window. Slowly it enfolded the house like a malignant cloud, gas seeping in through the windows.

Men were crawling back to the kitchen two by two, and Carter realized that there, they were assuming the submission posture to say their prayers.

Sidi removed his gas mask after the cloud had dispersed sufficiently. Twilight was coming on, and the Sidi pulled out two small boxes.

"Curiosity killed the cat," said the Sidi. "If he holds true to form, he will not wish to wait until it is completely dark."

He opened his boxes to display what he said were prototypes— small cameras, which, however, had night vision capabilities. He handed off one to Khalil, then asked Carter if he would like to look through the other. As he slipped the camera in front of him, the Sidi fixed the viewfinder to TWLT. Instantly the scene turned a garish green, by which he could see every feature clearly with no dimness.

"It's a wonderful tool for situational analysis," said the Sidi. "This is why I think they may try to advance before it is actually dark; he does not have these prototypes. Let us fire first and hit them first. We have the element of surprise."

Any doubts Carter had about the Sidi's tactics were beginning to lift, along with a bit of fuzziness created by liquor. He felt he had almost grown indifferent to the waiting.

I wonder if this is what the French call belle indifference.

If so, it only lasted briefly.

Now things began to move. By the light of the cameras, they were able to spot the movements of two out of the three men moving forward from cover to cover. Norway was, of course, the one remaining behind. Slowly, slowly, they drew closer.

Khalil was using Roulon's sniper rifle, which increased its visibility after sunset. Just as they were leaving the ranch, Roulon presented it to Khalil "for luck." The sight on it was remarkably clear.

"You may not wish to watch, Carter—it will be bloody," the Sidi told him.

"I might as well ride it out."

"Are you sure, honorable judge?" This was Kahlil at his elbow.

"Of course I'm not." But he stayed, and thought this action presented new knowledge for a judge.

He could not see what the men with night vision could, so he was startled when the Sidi said in a low voice, "Fire."

Two shots rang out. They were actually able to hear a slight bit of the impact when the two men hit the ground and lay there, dead.

This is how he made sure he got them.

It was indeed an unpleasant scene, and Carter hung back. His stomach had been in knots for hours; suddenly it relaxed and he made a beeline to the bathroom.

"Call the Rangers now," the Sidi told Khalil. "Soon there will be many people here and I would like you to be gone by then—I think Norway will try to flee by car. I will take care of things at this end."

The familiar whump, whump, whump of helicopter blades swiftly drew near. Khalil jumped into the chopper when it arrived, then they lifted off.

Shortly thereafter the scene was crowded. Police, Rangers, firemen, and the coroner filed into the scene.

"Let's get these boys off the scene before the journalists get here," said Roulon to the coroner.

The police cordoned off the house and the two corpses.

Roulon was the most advantageous arrival. He assisted filling in the particulars, and the licensing the Sidi acquired on his prior trip to Wellspring. The corpses were lifted into the coroner's van and driven away. The Sidi and his men disappeared. Officially there had been a fire. Carter was too tired to even think about obstructing justice.

"I am sorry about the house," Sidi said to Roulon. "Do you have insurance?"

"Don't worry."

The Sidi began speaking in Arabic to his men. Then he switched to English for Carter's sake. "Norway does not know about the helicopter. It left before the police arrived. Therefore, he is confident by driving his car, he will evade us."

The Rangers sent cars from distant points down the main highway route, but, although it was night, Khalil had his night vision from his World War 2 rifle. They would be able to search more swiftly than Norway could drive. This was not Nigeria, where the roads were terrible and there were no lines down the middle. This was a fast track for fast drivers.

In the sky, Bobby first traced the straightaway which had the nearest entrance ramp to them. "Once he gets on here, he will be unable to change cars!" he said to Khalil. Indeed, since it was night, traffic was considerably less dense. Picking out the rental car should be easy, but Bobby checked at every exit ramp.

After half an hour, they spotted him. They had to decide what to do. Should they notify cars on the ground? Khalil didn't think so.

"Go ahead of him, get down low, and get in front of him," he told Bobby, who looked at him somewhat questionably. Bobby had no idea what a remarkable shot Khalil was.

"Do you want me to run him off the road?"

"That won't be necessary. Just get me close enough to see him."

What is this guy up to? Thought the pilot.

Once ahead of Norway, Bobby lowered the chopper and turned 180 degrees the opposite way on the highway from Norway, until he sighted the rental car. "Now what?" he asked his passenger.

"Get as close as you can," said Khalil, who was wiggling out one foot onto the chopper landing railing. Bobby began to feel sweat dripping down his forehead. Khalil put one foot on the railing, and placed the other knee on the floor of the chopper, with the narrowly open door holding him in place. He waited as Bobby got closer, and sweatier. Then, without warning, Khalil fired right through the windshield, hitting Norway in the forehead. At this point the car lurched off the highway into the sagebrush.

Bobby contacted the nearest car, then set the chopper down. There was no doubt Norway had been killed.

Khalil said to Carter, "now you are free, honorable judge."

Back at the ranch, the men pulled in, a car in front with Sidi, Khalil and Carter, the rest of Sidi's men in a truck the ranch had loaned to them, all tired, hungry, thirsty, and exhausted. The Sidi pressed a plastic bottle into Carter's hand. "Drink some water. You are dehydrated."

A crowd of Herringtons surged toward them. Even Mabel noticed a crowd surrounding the two cars, and asked Karen to take her outside to see what was going on.

"Oh, Carter!" cried Valerie. "Is it over?"

"Yes, Val." He was too exhausted to say more.

"Thank God."

She stopped close to him.

"I am so glad," she said quietly.

CHAPTER 13

The next morning, Carter slept late. His mentality was stifled, and his body was exhausted. He ate breakfast, found a newspaper, and started reading—especially the part about a fire on Wellspring property, then fell asleep. For the rest of the day all he did was sleep, eat, and drink water.

The next morning, when he awoke, he found Valerie in the same room, in the wing backed chair, still in her riding gear, reading the same newspaper.

"It's certainly not the *Times*," she said with a smile.

"I plan to save it," he said, returning her smile." I weighed myself. I lost seven pounds."

"You'd better start eating before you have to buy a new wardrobe.'

"I want to thank you for all your assistance."

"I can't tell if we are still friends or not."

"I was trying to spare you my anxieties."

"How nice."

She's still miffed that I did not tell her the plan. I didn't know it myself.

"Valerie, I had no idea what the Sidi's plans were. I went through them I must say, unknowing what the plan was. But there definitely was one, and it was a masterstroke. Only two shots were fired the entire day.

"He had all Norway's tactics registered and was ready to play against them, in order to bring a solution without any gunfight battle."

"Why did you think he felt such a showdown was warranted?"

"Well, Val, the case was not completely over. Sanderson could still run part of the operation from prison, as long as there are rights for them to communicate with the outside world. He could still order a hit on me from there."

"Wasn't he the center of the spider web? Wouldn't it collapse without him?"

"Yes, he was, but facing a long time—perhaps a long enough time to die in prison—he faces an identity crisis between who he had been and who he is now, and whether or not he is still able to give orders. The refineries he supplied will be looking for a new middleman."

"You have seen this happen?"

"Yes, Valerie, of course I have."

"I can relate to that."

"Who do you feel you are now?"

"Dust in the hand of God."

"Does this mean you feel you have vacated your own personality?"

"Only you would be wise enough to ask such a question, Carter."

"I observed that all these fellows were protecting me—as well as themselves of course—but that I was not worthy of such a sacrifice. Yes, Valerie, it did change my perception of myself, although it will take time to work it out. But I know who *you* are."

Just then, Buddy appeared. "Sis. I've got a spectral on the telephone."

Valerie jumped up. She ran into his office. When she came out, she ran around the house picking up paraphernalia, including her Bible, bristling with page stickers.

"What is it?" Carter demanded.

"A spectral," she said, heading for a car.

He came after her. "What is that? I want to come with you. I feel this is going to show me something I have only had as words before!"

"You'd only be a hinderance, Carter!"

"No, I won't. There has to be something I can do, if only to observe."

"It is dangerous."

"So was yesterday."

Carter ran after her and got ahead of her, and leaned against the driver's side of the car, blocking her.

"Let's not repeat my error," he said.

She walked around to the passenger side, got in, and began to slide into the driver's seat, but Carter beat her there.

"Carter. Why are you acting like this?"

"Valerie, I—I want to go with you, as I sense this has something to do with that subject you turned me onto in *Screwtape?*"

"Are you referring to the devil?"

"I am."

"Well, then, this woman has been cursed, and her obituary is appearing on her television screen."

"Good Lord!"

"Only people who have no fear or sin can help in the process. And the devil can use personal sin against the process."

"I see."

"You can understand why you would be a hinderance?"

"I'm afraid so."

Valerie sat quietly, waiting for him to vacate her car. Then, suddenly, she started. "Oh! I just realized about sin! You've just been baptized! You have as clean a slate as you ever will have!"

"How timely!"

She added, "I realize you were just trying to be a gentleman. I doubt Lord Chesterfield might have had a remedy for this one," she replied.

"Could you…"

"Forgive you? Of course. "

"May I…drive you?"

"As long as you don't try to talk to me. I need to gather my wits."

He opened the driver's side door and got in, then started the car. *Thank God I've driven in France so this side of the road is comfortable.*

"One thing—where are we going?"

"Oh, right!" Valerie laughed and gave him the directions. He put the car in gear. Nevertheless, he had the uneasy sense of not being held into the earth by any of its geography, just a flat road that stretched to eternity, with mountains far away in the distance, and little vegetation that grew tall anywhere. Valerie withdrew into herself, he could perceive, communicating with something. *This is definitely going to be somewhere I have never been. Don't let it get to you.* (He had plenty of experience at that). He began to focus on repeating things he memorized to quiet his mind. *All rise…* Oh, yes. It worked. It always had.

What if he were about to encounter some entities he could not see? *Watch her.*

He drove into a small town, one that had no shops or public buildings, merely adobe houses, with wooden beams protruding at the roof line. Valerie signaled where he should pull over. He stopped the car and sat.

Then she produced the Bible she was carrying, which was bristling with book marks. "Here, Carter, the blue stickers relate to passages one can read about the devil. I want you to try to just keep reading them aloud. Can you try that."

"Of course."

"And you won't forget…"

"If I become afraid, I leave."

"The first thing to read is John 1, 1-10."

Valerie put her hand on his arm and said, "Remember, Lord, 'your wickedness is removed, your sin is purged!'"

He followed behind her as she knocked at the door, which was opened immediately by a distraught, dark-skinned, dark-haired woman with children huddled behind her skirts. She spoke to Valerie in a combination of English and Spanish. They stepped aside as Valerie and Carter entered.

"Why don't you show me the way," Valerie said. The woman made her way into what seemed to be the largest, common room of the house. The television was turned on, and it displayed the woman's obituary.

"It knows we're here," she told Carter, who was still staring incredulously at the screen. "Are you ready to read?" she asked. He nodded. Putting on his reading glasses, he read what she had told him to first—'In the beginning was the Word'—then he decided to open to the nearest bookmark, and read Valerie's underlinings: 'How you have fallen from the heavens, O morning star, son of the dawn! How you have been cut down to earth…In your heart you said, I will scale the heavens, Above the stars of God, I will set up my throne… I will ascend above the tops of the clouds, I will be like the Most High, No! Down to Sheol you will be brought, to the depths of the pit!'

At first his voice wobbled slightly, but before she had time to glance at him, it steadied, and he assumed his court judge's voice.

He flipped the pages: 'I saw Satan fall like lightning from the sky.' That sounded good enough to be read more than once!

As he read, she began to pray. "In the name of Jesus Christ of Nazareth, Satan…*God the woman was made of steel! Are my glasses dirty? She seems a bit fuzzy, almost as if she were beside herself.* He looked over the glasses frame, but the illusion persisted. To one side, the woman and her children were praying the rosary. Carter noticed a cessation of the passing of time, as if all that was happening was totally present. He had no idea how long they had been there.

Then, to his surprise, Valerie started sobbing. The boy ran over to her and gave her a Kleenex. "Ladies always cry," he announced.

Outside he thought he heard a car stopping. The creak of the door opening and shutting was followed by the sounds of footsteps. Jack Tottle had arrived. Carter glanced at him questioningly, startled by Valerie's tears. Jack simply smiled, went over to her, handed her a handkerchief, and removed an old crucifix from his side pocket. At the sight of it, Valerie stopped crying and smiled.

Suddenly Carter began to have the same sense he had as a judge, namely, that they were beginning to push in a definite direction, in the same way he could sense a prosecutor's attack beginning to fade before the defense's argument, or vice versa, when he sat on the bench.

Carter found what he considered to be a strong passage: 'the Son of God came for the very purpose of undoing the devil's work,' and to his surprise, found himself repeating the same verse as Jack was repeating.

Jack stood in front of the woman, holding up the crucifix and pronounced, "Hear me, abominable creature of the pit, the gates of hell cannot prevail against the church." Valerie placed a hand on Jack's shoulder, and this linking appeared to strengthen their prayers.

The television began developing static.

Valerie asked the woman, "have you ever practiced witchcraft?"

"Oh, yes, long ago!"

"Have you ever repented?"

"No! Should I?"

"Indeed," added Jack.

"I am sorry, Jesus, for I have sinned," she began, then launched into the Catholic *confiteor*.

When she finished, the television set suddenly regained its normal programming.

"Is it over?" Carter asked.

"Almost," Jack replied. He sat down on the sofa, and the woman handed him a glass of lemonade. Then she handed one to Valerie, and one to Carter. They both sat down.

Another car stopped outside, and Buddy came in.

"Buddy! All right! Search time!" Jack announced.

The two men commenced by rolling back the rug. On the back they found little pieces of paper with symbols on them, and Jack handed one to Carter, telling him it was a sign of witchcraft. Startled, Carter attempted to hand it back to Jack, who assured him it was safe to handle now. They looked behind the pictures and found more, and Valerie, taking the kitchen, found many more of them in the kitchen cabinets.

Jack then asked the woman, "Do you know of anyone with a grudge against you?" She halted. Finally she whispered, "My cousin. She hates me because I won't give her money to fix up her house."

"Did your family practice witchcraft?"

"Oh, yes, I was too, Pastor Jack, before I was converted."

Jack explained to Carter, "She would have gone to a priest if there were one near enough by."

"Now you have no need to worry. You've closed the channel," he told her. "Now some of it may land on her, possibly. Give me her telephone number." When his call was answered, he lapsed into Spanish. The voice on the other end was so disturbed they could hear it clearly, but had to wait for Jack to translate.

"It's too fast for me," Valerie said to her brother.

"Likewise."

Jack hung up.

"What happened?"

"She said she heard a voice asking, 'Ada, do you think you are greater than I am?' and she asked, "No, who are you, Lord?" She turned around, and her book of spells had vanished. I told her to call me when she is ready to renounce her witchcraft."

They all sat down together, drank lemonade, and celebrated their victory. The children, who had been stuck to the spot from terror, now ran and jumped all over the room. Jack produced a few treats he brought for them. The little boy who had given Valerie the Kleenex, sat down, wedged tight against her. He already knew *la Signora*.

Once outside, Valerie said, "Carter, you must be exhausted. Let me drive."

"Tell me, Valerie, why did you cry?"

"I was pleading to God to remove this awful situation."

"I am a bit knackered." He scrunched into the passenger seat and pulled down the visor to keep the sun out of his eyes. "I am deeply beholden to both you and your family."

"You aren't beholden to either of us, Carter."

A few moments after she had started, he was asleep. Valerie had always thought him a methodical man, and no more than now, when she noticed he was clean shaven again this morning. *It will take him time to recover from all of this. It will take time for both of us to recover from this.* In the quiet of the car, with a sleeping Carter, Valerie felt the old bonds of friendship now had been strained into something new.

When they arrived back at the ranch, she shook him gently, and he started awake with a "WHAT?"

"We are back at the ranch," she reassured him gently. "Do you want to sleep it off a bit more?"

"Yes—no—I don't really know."

"Come on, I will help you up to the apartment."

"All right."

She opened the passenger door and helped him out. "Put your arm around my shoulder and we'll go up the stairs."

"All right." It readily demonstrated how tired he was that he did not object to anything. He stumbled once or twice on the way up. She grabbed the hand around her neck so he would not lose his hold on her.

"Here we go," she said, dumping him gently on his bed. She took off his shoes.

He was asleep again by then. She reached in her pocket book for her cell phone, and called over to the house to see who was there; could they send over one of Sidi's men?

"They are driving around, sightseeing," her brother told her.

"He's really all in."

"I don't doubt it. Do you want me to come over?"

"To tell you the truth I'm also half asleep," she replied. Buddy appeared shortly, bringing his cell phone from his office so he could continue business.

It was in the middle of that night before Carter woke up hungry. Opening the refrigerator, he found several left-over sandwiches, which, in his current stage of hunger, he found very palatable. Before he went to sleep again, he remembered that Valerie had brought him upstairs; it was certainly the first time he had been so-helped by a woman; he had not felt a bit insecure. She was a woman who worked out of doors. Carter began to feel that he was beginning to emotionally thaw out.

"I'm beginning to feel a mite of relief," he told Valerie. "As if something like this will ever go away!"

"Some things never do."

"Was I of any help back at that house?"

"You were perfect."

"And you?"

"Whenever I think I might have gotten close to being perfect, along comes a nightmare."

"You can only control the conscious mind."

"I can't even do that. I was a wreck while you were out at the *caporal* house. Actually, I'm glad you didn't see me that way. It would not have helped you."

"I didn't realize it had affected you."

"Are you kidding? I was a wreck. I kept shaking. I was OK when it was far away, but as we came closer, I began to tremble. All I could think is what would Adrian think if I managed to get his best friend killed."

"I felt much the same way about seeing you. I had no desire to be killed because it would upset you. It did help understand the state of mind of defendants much better, I should say. On television they are all smart asses."

"I rode around all day so no one could see the state I was in. However do you deal with this every day?"

"It isn't happening to me, Valerie!"

"But—weren't you—sort of—imprisoned?"

"No doubt about it. I was. But not as severe as with a criminal."

"Are you in a hurry to get back to London?"

"No, I would rather like a bit of time to enjoy my surroundings!"

"I'm afraid Stella and Mercy may want to come out next week. Would that spoil things for you?" *I'm sure he doesn't want to deal with children.*

"I don't think they'll want to have much to do with me."

"Maybe not Stella, but not Mercy. She's curious about this mysterious godfather."

"I remember Adrian telling me once that Stella could be a little bitchy."

"He was right."

"I think I might like to have a chance to get to know Mercy."

"I'm afraid she will feel the same—I hope not enough to make a pest of herself."

CHAPTER 14

There were still three days before the girls arrived.

There was something Valerie wanted him to see.

I wonder what this is?

"I could put you on a horse and lead you, but then you'd be eating off the mantlepiece."

"Beg pardon?"

"Your butt will be sore."

"Frankly, Valerie, I do not foresee a horse in my future."

"City boy!"

"I am what I am."

"Mercy rides a pony while she is here."

"I shall watch her with admiration. I have had time to think, Valerie. I can see this as a positive…hopefully. Perhaps she won't take to me. All this, by the way, certainly rests on your approval. I wouldn't be underfoot that much—I am only off weekends and between sittings."

"By no means. You know we did raise our children as Christians."

"I assume that fact is included in the term 'godfather,' although I must admit I did not comprehend that then. You can fire me any time you want."

"Never tell that to a person with a hot temper."

"I've never seen you lose your temper!"

"Yes, you have."

"I think I can handle that. You've never seen what can happen in court."

"Adrian could handle it, too. We would walk it off."

"I'd be disappointed if he wasn't. Where is it you wish to go with me?"

"Let's get the jeep."

Not too much scenery flowed by as they four-wheeled along for half an hour. Then they came upon what appeared to be the ruins of an old chapel, and Valerie stopped. They both got out.

"This is probably the biggest secret of my life," she told him.

Walking through the door—which was not a door anymore, but an open space—Valerie said, "Stop here. I want to be sure there aren't any rattlesnakes in here."

"No! Isn't that dangerous?"

"I have on my snake boots."

He hadn't noticed her boots—new to him, not Valerie. She disappeared inside and he could hear her rattling and shaking things. "All clear!" she called. He came through the door and waited a moment for his eyes to adjust to the dimness after the blazing sunlight. Once his eyes had adjusted, he saw the ruins of an altar, with a crucifix hanging high above it.

"This is a Roman Catholic chapel?"

"Yes, it was."

"And—?"

"A priest lived here named Juan Carlos Montoya. He had been exiled—ordered—out here, because he thought the devil was an actual being. At that stage, the church was all about getting rid of superstitious and turning to science. He was a thorn in their side—Spanish people kept coming to him."

"He is the man who taught you." *Of that, I'm sure.*

"Yes."

"And how do you view the church that put him here?"

"I'd better be silent on that one."

"Do you children know about it?"

"Only Adry."

"Did Adrian?"

"Adrian couldn't handle evil."

"You astound me."

"How do you think he was always so bright and cheery? And believe me, none of us ever minded, because he shed who he was with all of us. He had no dark corners of his mind."

Neither of them spoke on the way home—both were thinking their own thoughts.

To their surprise, when they returned, the Gulfstream had returned from New York with Mercy and Stella, earlier than expected. Mercy ran toward Valerie yelling, "Mommy!" and shinnying up her like a tree. *I wonder how long she will be able to do that. This is a try-out for Mercy and me.*

As the party came over the mound, Carter hung back nervously. When Valerie placed Mercy back on the ground again, she took her hand, and came over to Carter.

"Mercy, this is your godfather, Carter."

Before he could move, she said, "oh!" and ran off toward the barn.

"I'm afraid we startled her."

"What shall we do?"

"Just go about our business."

Then, by providential timing, the Sidi and Khalil arrived back. They had taken the other six of their men to the airport at Abilene. Mohammed had taken someone at Texas A .and M. up on a chance to view their veterinary clinic.

The four of them were joined by Roulon as they sat outside. Mercy knew her grandfather, and jumped into his lap. "Howdy, granddaughter," he said. She gave him a kiss on the cheek.

Mercy sat down between Carter and Valerie, who each had their own chair.

Carter just held still. Roulon charged in to the gap. "I understand your godfather is here. How nice you get to meet him." She glanced toward him for the first time, but proved unsure.

"Who are these guys?" Mercy asked, looking at the Sidi and Khalil.

"They are friends of Carter's," said her mother, using the judge's name again.

"They are guest of ours," Roulon added. This presented a unified front.

Karen appeared with a tray full of lemonade, and Mercy greeted her, too.

"Where do you come from?" she asked the Sidi.

"From Arabia, little one."

"Are you just gonna call me *that?*"

"Not if you dislike it. "

"No, I think I like it."

And henceforth, that was what he called her.

Now Stella hove in to view and joined the party. "I'm the one that's going to be an actress!" she announced.

"Oh," said the Sidi, "where are you studying?"

"I'm not. Yet."

"Pardon my curiosity. I have two daughters who are professional dancers."

"Oh, where do they dance?"

"So far, only private parties," said Sidi, firmly. "But they want to dance out, but that is what parents are for. We are at a stalemate. I have promised them that if they allow one of my men to go with them, they can go. Of course they don't want that!" he said with a laugh.

How easily he talks to children.

Soon the group was enmeshed in conversation about entertainment, and Mercy lost being the center of attention.

Carter took a deep breath and abruptly asked her if she would like to take a walk. He waited while she was thinking. Her mien was as serious as Carter had ever seen on a child.

Finally, under the circumstances, this sounded like an escape to her. He stood up and she came over to him. They strolled along, quietly, each of them with a different set of worries.

This is not going well.

They came to a log on the ground, and Carter asked her if she would like to sit down. She began to hum.

"Would you like to go back?"

"Mister Carter, I've been thinking what I could call you. Have I met you before?"

"I saw you when I visited your home."

"Oh. You see, the thing is, I had a very nice Daddy."

Carter reached into his pocket for his wallet, opened it, and flipped to a picture of himself and Adrian, standing together with rowing oars. "Do you recognize these two fellows?" he asked her, handing her the photograph.

"Is that…Daddy?"

"Yes, we were both thinner in our rowing days."

"Oh." She sat looking at the photograph.

He waited.

"What if I call you Poppy?" She asked.

He exhaled and said, "That would be just fine, Mercy."

"Where do you live?"

"I live in London, Mercy, and I am a High Court judge."

"That sounds important. Is it important?"

"A bit." He suddenly remembered he had a picture of himself taken by him in full regalia by her father in his wallet. "Look here," he said. "Your Daddy took this picture."

"What's that on your head.?"

"It's a wig, Mercy."

"Why do you wear a wig?"

"It's an old- fashioned tradition but we judges of the criminal court still wear them."

"Why are the robes red?"

Shall I be frank? "Because it's the color of blood, Mercy. In the old days, judges could send a prisoner to be executed, but no more."

"Oh!"

"I might as well tell you now instead of your learning it later."

"Do you think that a child should know it?"

"I don't really know, Mercy. You see, I have no children."

"Oh! That's too bad!"

"I agree with you."

"How old are you?"

"I'm in my late forties."

"Isn't that old?"

"Actually it's only middle-aged. Mercy, I have spent the last three years safe housed, which is why I haven't seen you. I even had to miss your father's funeral."

"Why were you safe housed?"

I'd better go slow here.

"To protect me from some bad men."

"Oh. What kind of bad men?"

"I think it might wait to be discussed until you are a bit older."

"Why? Because I am a kid?"

"Very much because you are a kid."

"I don't like that," said this little girl.

My first compromise with a kid!

"I don't like being a kid. People are always deciding what to tell me or not. Mommy says I am a bit more mature because of what we happened."

"I'll agree with that. However, I promised your Mummy if I didn't know what to do, I'd ask her—OK?"

"Poppy, do you want to be friends?"

"Of course."

"Then there are things *I* want to know!" stated this child firmly.

My first experience at frustrating a child. She sounds like a real Herrington.

Carter thought for a moment. *Here I am, negotiating with a six-year- old!*

"I will tell you, if you will let me tell your mother," he said, and silently crossed his fingers for luck.

"Don't you think I can keep a secret?"

"It's not a matter of that. Mercy, but a matter of how I relate to your mother. I must be honest."

"Well, I guess it has to be OK ?"

"They already know it, Mercy."

"So it is a grown up secret?"

"I'm afraid it is. There were men who were trying to kill me, Mercy. The two men sitting with your grandfather kept me safe. Very safe." *Out of seclusion and into the frying pan.*

"That's right, Mercy—I am treating you like an adult."

"That's a good idea!"

Carter looked at his watch. *This has been one of the longest half hours of my life.*

"Do you think we should go back?"

"I guess so," she said reluctantly.

"Yes, we should."

She stood up. When he stood up, she reached for his hand. *Thank God I seem to have been issued the right godchild.*

"You walk fast, but I can keep up," she said, beginning to skip while still holding his hand. "Did you visit us when I was little?"

"Yes, I did, Mercy. And your family brought you children to London the day I was knighted."

"Oh, are you a knight?

"Yes, I am, Mercy."

"Cool!!"

That's the best response I've ever gotten.

They came into the site where conversation was still ongoing with the same persons. Valerie's head was slightly bowed. *She must have been praying for me. Adrian, too, perhaps. I could not have achieved this on my own.*

He again noticed the Sidi's social skills, as he asked, "Well, little one, have you had good walk?" Neatly defecting all the attention from Stella.

Valerie's head went up and he saw a big smile. *Of course she worries about the little one.*

At suppertime, the dining room boasted a large table, although there were smaller ones elsewhere in the house. Carter decided it would be beef for dinner. Mercy sat between him and Valerie.

Stella was across the table from them. At one point, Mercy asked if she could have more potatoes, and Stella announced loudly, "Of course she would want something so someone would have to get up and get it, the little pest!"

Mercy was stunned, then she began to cry. Carter stood up and came to her chair.

"Come on Mercy, put your arm on my shoulder," and he picked her up and carried her to the dimly lit living room, and plopped them both down on a sofa.

"I am not a pest," she snuffed.

"No, you're not, it's your sister." Carter had already found the button for the kitchen, and he pressed it; a voice asked what he wanted. "A new dinner for Mercy," he replied. While she was eating, Valerie came and they sat down out of earshot of Mercy. They spoke in quiet voices.

"Valerie, I don't want to butt in, but your daughter is behaving exactly like a person who needs a strong set of limits."

"Really?"

"In court we say a barrister is trying to lead a witness. It always happens when a barrister faces a new judge. He'll try it, to see if he can get away with it."

"We've always tried to cater to her."

"I think you are heading in the wrong direction with it."

Valerie sat and absorbed this new idea. Then she excused herself and went back to the dining room and sat down. Stella was still on her high horse, complaining about her sister, and how children that little should not we allowed at the supper table.

"Stella," said her mother.

"Yes?"

'That's not the way we raised you. Stop it."

Stella's eyes widened, then she jumped up from the table and flounced out of the room.

Roulon asked, "Anyone want seconds?"

Unexpectedly, Mabel, who was sitting at his right, said "I would, dear."

"What do you want honey? I'll get it for you." He picked up her plate and went into the kitchen himself.

The next morning, Stella told her mother she was taking a car to go into town.

"No, you're not— not until you apologize to your grandfather for messing up his dinner, and –to your sister."

"Then I'm not going to go!"

Valerie said, "Suit yourself." *Three cheers for Carter.*

CHAPTER 15

What a day, Valerie thought. Amazing to see Carter deal with both my daughters. This guy with no experience with kids. Maybe being a judge, he has learned something.

Whatever other feelings Valerie may have felt for him, she carefully squashed. But she did notice that wherever she went on the ranch, sooner or later—mostly sooner—he would show up. And that she was glad when he did.

One day when they were sitting on the porch, suddenly he asked, "Valerie, would you marry me?"

What?"

"You heard me!"

"I did—but I am rather—shocked."

"You must admit we get on rather well."

"Yes, we do, but as just friends, I thought. I didn't realize…"

"We have been friends for some time now."

"Yes, we have."

"What kind of reservations might you have about marrying again?"

"Well, I don't know how to put it—"

"It must be sex."

Unexpectedly, Valerie blushed.

"You need not worry, I do read, and I understand that a widow in a second marriage may feel, sexually, that she is being unfaithful to her late husband. I'm not sure that would be so, as both you and I love Adrian."

"I don't know if I would feel that or not, but I suppose I must, since they write articles about it."

Then, there was a pause.

"Carter, you may be right about sex, but not for the right reason. I must really ask you—you have been a bit of a variety man—do you really propose to settle down with one person?"

"Two persons."

"You include Mercy?"

"Yes, I do. I don't think you'd be happy without her."

"What about you?"

"How could I not love her, she's part of Adrain."

"Do you think you are able to do that? I'd like to know without any lies if this is your real intention. At this age, I hardly want a divorce."

"I've lived for three and a half years without any sex, Valerie."

"Yes. By necessity."

This is going to be tough. But I deserve it.

"Actually, I have no doubt they could have provided me a woman," he said boldly.

"Well, you did, didn't you?"?

"No, because it was not by my choice. I am that egotistical, Valerie. I am not a saint; I preferred self-satisfaction."

"But that was because of a unique situation, Carter. I must admit, I wasn't thinking along those lines, but more, whether you simply wished to find soft place to land, as if you were-- as it were-- retiring from the field."

"Much more than that, Valerie my Valerie. You were my best friend's wife. It took me a while to get to know you because of course you were an American! Eventually I did understand you. I could talk to you. I did realize you were someone unique in my life, you were very open. Adrian died and I was safehoused. Three years of reflection gives a man a chance to really look at himself. Nate said it was the best thing that ever happened to me."

"And what was the result?"

"I have both been a bit juvenile and a bit scared stiff of another Norah. And I must admit, I have been more influenced by my father's attitudes than I ever realized, because I didn't really look, I simply preserved a hard shell and the rest—was pushed underneath. They were unconscious reactions."

"It was lonely being unable to see the lot of you. I realized I'd lost my safe haven, where I could be myself. You can't imagine what a shock it was to see you in court. It was as if life had walked back in through the door. I don't know what happened, although I imagine you do—except to say, I began to live on another level. And you and Adrian were the only two people I knew who lived there, except for your family."

Adrian…the breakthrough! "What about the children?"

"I've known them the best of all the children I've known, not to mention I've been taken by Mercy. And not to mention, you could use a bit of aid with Stella."

"That's below the belt!"

"Not really."

"I need a bit of time to think this all over."

"Yes—take it."

"How would you like to see an Indian trading post?"

"That sounds interesting." *That is closing the door for the moment.*

After around thirty miles, there was a large sign with an Indian chieftain in full head dress, with the sign ' trading post.' She stopped at a pueblo type building—artificially produced. Inside, where there was an explosion of turquoise. There were bracelets, belt buckles, wrist watch bands, pottery—it took Carter a while to assimilate it all. He was able, even without the ability to judge color, to appreciate various patternings on the pots and decided to buy one after asking Valerie what colors it sported. "Grey and white," she retorted. "Very nice."

Once back outside, Carter asked, "Am I going to see a reservation?"

"Why would you want to?"

"Isn't it part of the ambiance?"

"I'm not sure I'd call it that, Carter." She turned left onto a dirt road, and the land Carter saw was somewhat derelict as far as growing anything; there was an occasional dwelling that was ramshackle, and he asked her, "Is this it?"

"Yes, you are seeing one end of the trail of tears."

This meant she needed to explain history to Carter, who was, of course, aware of the American response and rejection of slavery, but not of the plight of American Native Americans.

However, as they proceeded and came up to one dwelling, a woman waved Valerie down, and she lowered the window to talk. It appeared some discussion was going on about a doctor visit the woman could not afford. Valerie began to root in her purse, then quit with an expression of disgust.

"Do you have your wallet with you?"

"Of course."

"With American dollars?"

"Of course."

"Would you give me what you have? I'll pay you back."

"Don't bother."

He reached into his jacket pocket. "Here you are." There were several hundred-dollar bills and Valerie gave it all to the woman, who thanked her.

"Let me know what comes of your doctor's visit," Valerie said, as they parted.

Carter puzzled for a few moments. "Roulon hasn't gotten out here?" he finally asked.

"Nothing formal," said Valerie. "Otherwise he'd have to deal with the Bureau of Indian Affairs."

After a few more miles, Valerie pulled over to the side of the road. "I'm sorry. Perhaps I was too harsh with you this morning."

"You did give fair warning you can be angry, Valerie."

Back came memories of Adrian. She was trying to figure out what room to sleep in, and she tried them all. Then someone told her to attempt to sleep on Adrian's side of the bed. From then on, she began to sleep again.

There they were, father, mother, and son in the family cemetery. Sometimes she wished it were not back of the house, because one was often aware of its presence, yet it seemed to emit a magnetic pull, and she always wound up sitting on the ground beside Adrian. For months, she would only get out of bed to stagger down to her studio, and sink into a reclining chair there. The familiar table, stained with paint, covered with bottles of powdered pigment, different-sized brushes, a small stove for making gesso from scratch with a fire extinguisher above it, a small refrigerator in which to store eggs and a rack for them to sit upon as they came to room temperature, and an easel facing a large window completed her arrangement.

"No matter where I live, I shall have to have a studio. Or rent one."

"I hadn't thought that far ahead."

"You see, I don't know if transferring to another studio will throw off my art work."

He was momentarily silent. Then he asked. "Consistent with your necessity, what would it involve?"

"Good light. Lots of it! A wooden floor. No carpeting. I don't want to have to worry about spilling paint on it. I am not sloppy except in my studio.

"You must understand my arrangements with my family. I've been turning out stickers for them to put on their beef so in the family distribution system, I've moved from a passive stockholder to an active one. It pays much better! You see, this is the one thing that has remained stable in my life; if I lose that—I'm afraid I lose myself."

Carter was strangely moved by this conversation, for he couldn't remember having this degree of concern for another woman other than his mother. This was a cry of the heart, and he heard it as such. Until just then, he had not allowed himself to realize how much he cared about her.

"I'm not sure I have the faith to start over again," she said.

"You are forgetting something. I intend to help you."

"I thought you'd be much too busy."

"Val, I am not wedded to the High Court."

"What do you mean?"

"I could always go back to being a barrister. For one thing, I'd make more money!"

"I don't think I would be happy to see you do that."

"Why?"

"Let's just say I respect your accomplishments. I wouldn't want you to take a step backwards."

"You are very thoughtful. We could always leave London between sittings."

"But we would be tied down. We'd have to stay while Mercy is in school."

That is in present tense.

"But the most important question, Carter—how would you feel having the devil around the house from time to time? He can cause a bit of nuisance."

"Give me an example."

"Fooling about with electricity. Things vanishing--and usually reappearing, although not always. Mainly affecting communications, by machines or without them."

"How did Adrian deal with it?"

"He didn't."

"What?"

"You know him. He could never admit the presence of evil. That is why he was always so cheerful! "

"Yes, I suppose it must have been."

"Adry is a mix of both of us, poor lad!"

"I hate to tell you this, Valerie, but I felt perfectly natural at that woman's house. I felt as though I was finally arriving at some place I was supposed to be."

"Oh."

There was a silence.

It's true. She's thinking about that one.

Arriving back at the ranch after dinner, he asked, "Shall we take a walk?"

"That's a nice idea." She took Carter's arm. Looking up at the night sky, she asked if he knew anything about the stars.

"Only what my Mum taught me—mind you, we couldn't see much of the night sky from where we lived!" *What a relief to be able to say something about my early life.*

Then suddenly, a short burst of lightning—and only one—a lambent light. It flashed and disappeared.

Uh Oh, she thought. *A sign.*

CHAPTER 16

On their return to the ranch, they sat down on a bench in the darkness.

"Have you thought any further about our conversation this morning, Val?" He asked, took her hand, and kissed it.

He's always called me Valerie.

"My *cavaliere servante!*" She said.

He burst out laughing. "That doesn't exactly go with my background."

"Or mine," she replied. *That's the first time I've really heard him have a good laugh.*

"We are both from below the salt."

"Have you considered the fact I wouldn't exactly be the kind of wife for a High Court judge?"

"What's more important, I do not need to put on a front."

"I guess that's true."

"Indeed it is, my dear Val," he said, surprising her with saying it in a Cockney accent.

'Are you sure it wouldn't put a dent in your career?"

"On the contrary, I think they would be happy to have me married off. The court is a conservative place."

"I hope so—either for me or someone else."

"How remarkably evasive."

"Carter, after what happened to me, I am fearful."

"I was fine with my last health checkup."

“So was Adrian.”

“But I receive a pension, Valerie. It’s not the same situation.”

“I didn’t mean it financially. It’s about closeness.”

“I am all for it. After my safehousing, I experienced what it is really like to be alone. As well, I must tell you, in that woman’s house, reading out the passages you marked, I actually felt I’d arrived at some place I was meant to be.”

I thought so.

“Would you want an engagement?” he asked.

“I think I was going to say I’d give it a try. But how much would we really learn? We already know each other well.”

“No, I don’t really fancy you nor I driving 8 hours every weekend.”

“I could rent a flat in London for a while, but I think that would be a waste of money.”

Never forget that she’s a Herrington. She can make up her mind!

“I would be stepping out in trust.”

“Never go out for a hamburger when you have a steak at home.”

“What?”

“Quoting Paul Newman.”

“That’s a good enough analogy for someone who raises beef,” she replied. She stifled a yawn.

“Ready for bed?”

“I’m afraid so.”

“I’ll walk you over.” He was still holding her hand. At the door, he asked, “Might I kiss you, Val?”

“I guess so…yes.”

Carter was three inches taller than Valerie, so he bent down while she stood up on her toes.

He gave her a gentle kiss; next, they looked at each other. Suddenly they were overwhelmed by whatever it was that was happening. She threw her arms around his neck, and he lifted her against him slightly. She could feel his arousal and he pulled her closer.

What say you, my lady…

“What say you we do skip being engaged,” he murmured.

"O, yes," she whispered in his ear.

Neither of them wanted to let go, so they held each other. Finally, they parted.

"How do you want to handle this?" he asked her in the morning.

"A thousand dollars and a ladder," she replied.

"Low key?" he replied.

"I guess I need—we need—to tell father."

"As you wish."

This would not be like her first, young marriage, with all the fanfare and falderal, gown, church, bridesmaids. No. A widow and a highly accomplished middle -aged groom.

They found her father alone in the breakfast room, reading his newspaper.

"Dad, the Judge and I are going to get married," she said.

Looking amazingly unsurprised he looked up over the paper. "I've got eyes," he replied.

"Really?"

"I've got eyes. Tell you what. Why don't I announce it at dinner tonight. Save you some trouble."

"Indeed it will," Carter answered.

He went back to finishing his paper.

"He took that awfully well," she said to Carter, once they were outside.

"He's got as position to uphold. He is the calm at the center of the storm," Carter replied.

Once alone, Roulon said a prayer of thanksgiving.

"There's one other person we ought to tell before tonight," she said.

"Mercy?"

"Yes, She'll be upset otherwise." *He's getting into the hang of children.* "What about Stella?"

"She'll act as if I'm to be the bride of Frankenstein."

Outside, Valerie took a quarter out of her pocket and said, "I'll flip you for who has to tell her."

"Don't bother, I will do it."

I'm not sure I like that. "Why don't we both tell her?"

"That's the spirit."

Mercy was outside, waiting for someone to saddle the pony Roulon kept for the smaller children. Carter walked right up to the animal's nose in what he felt might be an intimidating fashion, but Mercy announced, "Watch out, Poppy, ponies love to nip!"

"Poppy?" asked Valerie.

"I asked the judge if I could call him that, and he said yes."

"Mercy, can you keep our secret until tonight—Grandpa wants to tell everyone that we are getting married."

"OK!"

The man saddling her horse was finished and was calling her. She skipped off; Carter knew enough now to know that when she was happy, she skipped.

"Valerie," he said, "I have a question. The place to marry is usually the bride's discretion, I believe—would you wish to marry here?"

"Could we do it before we go back to England?"

"Let us borrow your father and go in to the license bureau."

"Oh—you mean—"

"I'm sure he has a bit of local clout."

Upon reaching city hall, they debarked from the car, Roulon taking a bit more time to get his right leg out, then, when he grabbed his cane, they proceeded to the licensing office, which, it being a small town, was only a few steps.

"Mr. Herrington!" said the clerk.

"Good morning, son! Let's see if you can whip us up a marriage license ASAP."

Assuming, and rightly so, since this was a public office, the telephone would not be limited to local calls, Carter, using his prepaid international calling card, proceeded to dial off a long string of numbers, which, apparently, connected him to some archive in London, where he asked for his birth certificate to be e-mailed to him using a "visitors" password. It came and he asked to use the computer, and programmed in his 'visitor' request, then printed out the certificate.

"Excellent! May I suggest you also go down the street for your blood tests."

Walking along with her father, Valerie was becoming accustomed to the stamp of his cane, which was new to her. *He and Mom are getting up there.*

At the infirmary, they encountered the doctor, who was among the section of humankind who took delight in frustrating the plans of the high and mighty. He took their blood then hurried out of sight downstairs. After half an hour, Carter got up, and asked at the desk, "May I use your phone?"

He dialed a string of numbers, and, at the other end, a voice said, "Nathan Levi."

"Nate," said Carter, "I need to tell you that I am being married on Saturday." A bit of discussion ensured, including Valerie saying, "Saturday?"

At this point, the doctor came storming upstairs, demanding to know who was holding up his phone line. Carter smiled and dialed off another string of numbers. Meanwhile, Valerie and the clerk waited to see what would happen next, which was that Adry answered at the other end.

"Adry, your mother and I are getting married Saturday. Here, I'll put her on." He handed her the receiver.

"We are?" Valerie asked.

"Always give them a deadline."

The doctor began to sputter and threaten to call the police.

"Please do," said Carter.

Roulon was beginning to smile.

Meanwhile the woman behind the desk whispered to the doctor, "That is Mr. Herrington, sir!"

"I don't care if it's God almighty, he can't tie up my phone line!"

"When you give us our blood tests results, I will give you back your receiver," said Carter, at his most pompous. Roulon was delighted. The doctor was beginning to note that Carter had a foreign accent, which told him he did not know what he was dealing with.

"Why don't you walk down to the police station?" Roulon inquired sweetly. "This man is a High Court Judge in England, and he is used to getting the documents he wants quickly."

The doctor realized he had met more than his match and slunk off back downstairs, allowing ten minutes to pass before he returned with the results. He was beginning to realize that his was a politically appointed office, and that Roulon Herrington was on the Board of the local hospital. Some people believed he *was* the Board of the local hospital.

Roulon said, "Honey, you send me the phone bill." He was used to tyrannical types who might try to stick the clerk with it.

Now, real planning began; Carter told Valerie that tactfully he should invite Adry to be his best man, but he really wanted to ask Khalil (and that was what he was going to do). He dialed Khalil's number, and explained what was happening; Khalil said he would be back there again by nightfall.

For the rest of the afternoon, Carter and Valerie sat on the bench, holding hands, and chatting happily.

The dining room was two stories high, but at the second-floor level, an oak floor was held up on columns which went around the lower dining room under the walkway, made by cutting out a portion of the second floor, with doors at either end, so a person on the second floor walkway could come down the stairway for dinner without having to come downstairs first. Space under the walkway contained chairs and a television set. The walls were white; the only color in the room other than the table settings was a series of stenciled risers, which Valerie had painted as a teenager.

Carter and Valerie seated Mercy between them.

Here it comes –father is starting to stand up. Once settled securely on his feet, Roulon tapped his fork against his glass to command attention. All eyes turned toward him.

"I'd like to propose a toast to a couple who are going to marry here on Saturday." He raised his glass. "To my daughter, Valerie, and her fiancé, Judge Carter Braxton." The table dissolved into a babble of vices and a few clapping hands.

"What is it, Roulon?" Mabel asked.

"Our daughter is getting married."

"She can't do that!" Mabel exploded. "She's already married! You tell them to stop that!"

"Sweetheart—" Roulon began. The table quieted before this display of a wandering mind.

"No, you listen to me! She can't do this!"

Valerie began to flush with anger. Quick as a flash, her sister-in-law, Buddy's wife, Karen, came to the head of the table. She put a hand on her mother-in-law's shoulder, and asked Mabel if she knew it was time for the cooking show they generally watched. Slowly Mabel turned away from Roulon to look up at Karen. Karen helped her up and they went off to watch television.

"Getting' so a man can't eat a meal in peace and quiet," said Roulon philosophically.

The next morning, Claudia burst downstairs, to state a point most relevant to her. *What were people going to wear?*

"I'm not sure, "said Valerie.

"Oh, Valerie, please please please don't thwart a clotheshorse! Let me pick out some dresses in Dallas and bring them back for you to try on."

"Oh, you really don't need to do that—"

"It's not need, I want to!" exclaimed Claudia. "Please."

In the end, Valerie gave in, but said to Carter, "I should have just said no."

"I'll fix it," he said, and went upstairs to talk to Khalil. A few minutes later, he came back downstairs. "Khalil suggests we go to Dallas—we can take their Gulfstream—and pick me out something for the occasion. Sidi will meet us there. That way, Val, dear, you can rest easy. Makes everyone happy."

Bless the man. He knows how to fix things.

Once in Dallas, the three of them proceeded to Neiman-Marcus. The sight of Mid-East customers—who even sometimes arrived with money stashed in paper bags—was very good business, so there was a bustle in their direction. The clerk brought forth several light weight suits of formal wear.

"Try on the one you like."

When Carter appeared out of the changing room, the Sidi tested the buttons to see what they were well-affixed, checked the sewed shut pockets to make sure they led into real pockets, looked at the cut of the shoulders and waist, and indicated small tailoring to be done with the tailor's chalk with which he made the appropriate marks. He then announced it would have to be done by this evening, as they were on their way elsewhere. Of course, such fast service would cost extra.

"Just give me the total," said the Sidi, who, to cement the deal, produced one of his rolls of cash and peeled off two packets of hundred-dollar bills, with rubber bands around each ten of them—a thousand dollars apiece. The clerk looked pleased to have engaged one of the mythic Mid- Eastern customers for real, for himself. Sidi always thought it was a nuisance that in America you could get no money above a hundred-dollar bill.

Khalil handed him a generous tip. *I guess he is the petty cash man!*

Now they went off the main streets onto a back street to which the Sidi navigated. "I've got the address of a really good jeweler," he said. Off they went to some back street, whose owner was perceptively Jewish.

Now, Khalil, to Carter's surprise, told the jeweler what they had come for in Hebrew. Carter walked up and down the cases, finding one he liked, brushed gold with tiny stones set right into the ring itself. *This looks to hold up under heavy wear and tear.*

Carter began to take out his wallet, but the Sidi preceded him. *Damn. I don't want another man to purchase it. Let me settle with him later and not turn things sour.* Carter handed the ring to Khalil, who said it would be as safe with him as if it were in Fort Knox.

The jeweler suggested several ethnic restaurants, and whatever it was that came, Carter found tasted delicious, as were the non-alcoholic drinks. *A wedding without a hangover,* Carter thought thankfully.

Back at the ranch, Claudia returned from her shopping trip with several hanging bags. Valerie shrank as she looked at them, when the one last produced for her attracted her: pale lavender outfit, a skirt that descended to the foot in tiers, a top covered with a peplum jacket. Carter knew he was not supposed to look at it.

Tomorrow—all this will be over, they both thought.

And sure enough, the next day, Saturday, was frantic. *Good thing it's at 11, or the lid might blow off the house.* Did they want to stay for a wedding brunch? Yes. You ought to let your hair down—and so saying, Claudia pulled out a bag of big hair rollers, washed Valerie's hair, toweled it, put in the rollers, lowered the headpiece of the drier, and plugged it into the wall. Valerie could only move two feet. Then came Grace, wanting them to OK the menu for the bunch.

What did they want to do after the service and brunch? "I haven't been able to think so far ahead!" she told him.

"What sort of place do you want?" Asked Carter, sitting down beside her as the hair drier hummed.

"Privacy! No noise! Buddy has an arsenal of fireworks for special occasions. We must leave the ranch!" Carter got out his laptop and began pulling up photos of hotels, rentals, beaches, dancing, and eating.

"There—that one!" said Valerie. "It's got private little houses!"

"I shall make the call," he responded, and he went in to the main house to use the land line phone.

"When will you be arriving, sir?"

"Where's the nearest airport?" It was a twenty -minute ride. "Can you send someone or must I call a taxi?"

"Let me ask." It was not for the desk clerk to make such decisions. He returned to report that their car was already involved in catering for a party, "although there will be a taxi or rental cars at the airport, sir." *This situation is not terribly obliging.*

Valerie upset Claudia by saying she would like a picture of the two of them before they left that ranch for the church. "Face it—we'll never look this good again!"

"But he'll see your dress!"

"He'd see it in an hour anyway!"

I'm glad she has no trouble bending the rules.

"Come on, honey, it's Val's day," added her husband, Charlie. "She gets like this at weddings."

"Carter!" Valerie yelled up the staircase to the apartment. As he stood next to her, Valerie, trained to notice detail, observed he was one of the rare breed who still tied his own bow tie. Meanwhile he took in the result of Claudia's handiwork; Claudia was busy with the drape of the skirt for the photos. He rarely saw Valerie's hair dressed and falling down, and it was beautiful in the sunlight.

Valerie was restless until Claudia said, "I usually get paid for this, you know!" And got a laugh from the bystanders.

Carter and Khalil left before Valerie and Mercy; the church was family only. Carter and Khalil finally moved toward the altar and stood waiting, Khalil resplendent in a magnificent robe of white and Zara thread, thread wrapped in gold.

For music, there was Jessica playing her guitar and singing "The Wedding Song." Carter was intrigued by the line, 'Woman draws her life from man and gives it back again.'

Halfway through the song, Roulon and Valerie started down the aisle, with Mercy, the flower girl, in front of them, scattering wildflowers. Carter reached for Valerie's hand. He knew the ceremony would bring back memories; when they arrived at the 'until death do us part;' indeed, Valerie wiped her eyes. Carter handed her his handkerchief., *I'm glad Jack Tottle is marrying us.* His first wedding had been at the recorder's office.

Although brunch was being served after the ceremony, Valerie was too keyed up to eat much, although Carter tried his second hot dog. After lunch they both went to change out of their wedding finery. Khalil also changed into his work clothes. Valerie made sure someone took color photos of the two of them standing together in their wedding finery.

Maybe I'll paint it later.

Once airborne, they sank back in their seats and waited for the adrenaline to wear off. Meanwhile, Khalil talked to London, and assured Carter that his cat Dulcie was all right.

Khalil brought the aircraft down at a smallish airport—small enough Carter wondered if he could make it, but of course he did. Khalil insisted on carrying both their suitcases to the cab stand. He then bid them goodbye, and Carter noted he was blinking a bit more than usual.

Once in the cab, unbidden, the driver began a travelogue of the places they passed, which, in a state of half-fatigue, they did not appreciate at all. Finally, Carter said to the driver, "Please stop the travelogue, my wife has a headache."

"What?" demanded the driver, not catching the words because of Carter's British accent.

"He said stop the travelogue I've got a headache," Valerie snapped.

"Sorry."

Stopping at the main building, they signed in, and a representative came out to guide them to their cottage. In the lobby they could hear noise from a party. The noise followed them outside, growing dimmer, but by the time they reached their cottage, it still could be heard.

Carter said, "Take us to one further down, we can still hear the music."

"Oh, I don't know that I can do that sir. It may already be booked."

"I don't see any lights on in it," Carter remarked. "Take us down there and we shall see."

"Oh, no, I must consult the main office," said the representative.

Carter pulled out his mobile phone.

"What are you doing, Sir?"

"I am thinking whether I should call our pilot and ask him to come back and get us."

As he expected, the threat of losing a sale was worse than booking them in to the wrong cottage. Down they went. Looking in the window, they saw no signs of inhabitation, but the representative did not have the right key to open the door. He said he'd return to the main house to get the key.

Valerie said to Carter, "someone's messing with us, Carter." She sat down on the porch steps, and pulled Jack's crucifix out of her purse.

"Where did you get *that?*"

"Jack gave it to me to take just in case—the devil loves to mess people up at big events. Sit down beside me." She raised the cross and instructed any evil spirits to move off.

The representative came back with the key, let them in, and sent their suitcases down.

Carter flopped on the bed. "Are you hungry?"

"Yes."

"Are you hungry?"

"Yes."

"Let's see if they have room service." They did, but it would cost extra. Taking a page from the Sidi's book, Carter said, "Just give me the total."

Valerie ordered an omelet and salad. "It's pretty hard to mess that up," she murmured.

Dinner arrived, and before they began to eat, Carter said, "Valerie, you have blessed me with a family just when chances of that were growing really rare."

"Why, thank you, Carter, I'm not sure how many men would feel that way!"

"Now, Valerie, didn't you once accuse *me* of being cynical?"

"Did I?"

"Let's take a shower together. I could use one."

"You had mineral water for dinner?"

"I did. New wine in new wineskins, dearest."

"You've been reading the Gospels?"

"I read them all waiting with the Sidi for Norway to come."

"Pretend we're in the Garden of Eden?"

"If you can imagine that. I'm not sure I could."

They sat down on the side of the bed, and asked for a blessing.

"I'll go first, you come when you're ready—or stay here if you're not," he told her. He went into the bathroom, turned on the shower, and she could hear his shoes hit the floor. She took off her shoes. She began to have a slightly panicky feeling, and worried about what to do with her hair, which was still hanging down in her wedding hairdo. She knocked on the bathroom door softly-too softly to be heard over the running water. She knocked a bit more loudly, and heard a "Come through!"

She opened the door a crack and said, "Carter, I am afraid I must wear a shower cap, otherwise I will have wet hair all night."

Carter's head popped out from behind the shower curtain and he replied, "I think I can deal with that, Valerie."

Leaving the door still open a crack, she took off her clothes, then——put on her slip again, and donned her shower cap.

"Here I come," she said. She took a quick look at the mirror: Woman in slip and shower cap. *Let's see if he can love this.* She took hold of the edge of the shower curtain and slid it back wide enough for her to get through; he handed her in, and responded as a normal man would to a half -naked woman who was gradually becoming more naked as the water clung to her slip.

People look so different without any clothes, she thought. She was pretty sure he was thinking the same thing.

His arms went gently around her back, and hers around his neck, while they stood facing each other, looking each other over, feeling the erotic potential between them rise. Then he took a step closer to her, and slipped slightly on the wet surface.

"Let's get the hell out of this bathtub!" he said.

Once on the dry floor, she divested herself of the wet slip; as she raised it over her head it knocked off her shower cap and her hair came tumbling down.

"Venus on the half shell!" said Carter.

Bottecelli. Of course. All his clothes are neatly folded. His underwear was under his clothing so she could not determine the always vexed question, briefs or boxers?

Wrapping a bath towel around her, Carter procured one for himself. "Come on. Let's sit on the bed."

He knows I'm feeling apprehensive.

Valerie's hair was still curled and hanging down, part down her back, and strands over her chest. Carter gave that strand a light, mischievous touch.

"What happens to this at night?"

"Oh—ah, I usually braid it. But tonight, I—just don't feel like it."

"And in the morning?"

"I brush it up and use my clip to fasten it to the top of my head."

"That part I'm familiar with," he said, with a smile.

"Sometimes I think I ought to cut it."

"Check with me first," he said.

Now there was a silence in which each wondered to do next. Slowly, Valerie twisted around to face Carter.

Then she said, "Carter? Hold me??"

"Now and forever."

CHAPTER 17

The days of accumulated vacation dwindled down; commensurately, Carter, who had now seen what ranching involved (lassoing cattle, bringing them into the corral, tying their feet together to be branded, cattle cutting, changing grazing ground and horse breaking) was beginning to experience an eagerness to return to his own occupation.

The Sidi had not attended the wedding, and they wondered why; but shortly thereafter, he returned, having been at a NASA ceremony, and bearing two GPS pins, one for Carter, one for Khalil, and demonstrated how they worked. The Sidi also gave him a photograph of 'the Virgin of Zeitoun,' so Carter could try to see a figure of a woman, more solid than ectoplasm, standing by a circular protuberance atop the church roof.

They would have to return as they came, by military transport, and Stella planned to ride home with Mercy on regular aircraft. However, she told her mother she wanted a change of pace, which involved staying with her grandparents. Diego would fly them all to New York, then return Carter and Valerie to Andrews Air Force base.

"You have to do as your grandfather says," her mother commented.

"Yes, he told me the moment I disobey him he will ship me back to you," she told her mother. But what about Mercy? Help came from Claudia, who announced she would ride to London with Mercy and do some shopping.

Carter did not have a double bed, so Khalil loaned him an air mattress. When all was quiet, Valerie said "Psst!" motioned him to climb in with her.

In the morning, they re-united with Mercy and Claudia at Carter's old flat atop the Sidi's building. After breakfast. Carter asked Valerie if he could borrow Mercy and show her his chambers. He took Mercy to his courtroom with him, which nearly caused a riot, as news that he had married filled his courtroom with incredulous colleagues.

"Yes, I have been released from safehouse, yes, I have been married, yes, I now have stepchildren, the youngest of whom, Mercy, is here with me!" He lifted her up to a bench at the prosecutor's station. She said, "Hi!" leaving her audience thunderstruck.

They were to stay at Carter's old apartment on the tenth floor until they found a rental. Carter's furniture—such as it was—was still in storage, and Valerie told him they had furnishings at Pendragon which could be theirs for the taking. "We keep a room stocked with things we have found that we like but don't have room for," she said.

Mercy immediately bonded with Carter's cat, Dulcie, who did not mind being picked up and carried around; she would squirm when it was time to put her down. A bedroom was set up for Mercy, and a new bed installed in Carter's bedroom. Dulcie had her own bed, but preferred to sleep on the bottom of the bed of one or the other of her persons.

This was their first impasse; Carter did not want a cat sleeping on their bed. At first, she was happy with Mercy, but she did view Carter as her main person, so she slowly crept back to the bottom of their bed. Carter kicked her off, and Valerie was upset. Bit by bit he adjusted to her sleeping on the outside of Valerie's pillow, but circumspectly vanished if any lovemaking was going on. Valerie said there was nothing so peaceful to drift off to sleep with as a cat purring by her ear.

One of the first things Carter wanted to do was a visit to Nate and Deborah. Valerie said she might wear her wedding gown; so Carter joined her in his 'gladrags.' Mercy decided to wear her flower girl dress.

Nathan Levi answered the door, and it was difficult to picture him at first because he and Carter threw their arms around each other, as Nate called to Deborah. When they unentangled, Nate revealed himself to be of medium height, slightly stooped with age; his skin was marked with the passing hand of time. His hair was balding on the top, with hair combed over his bare spot. He, too, was dressed for the occasion with a velvet smoking jacket, his best pair of trousers and elegant slippers.

Deborah wore a modest dress and flats, and neatly coiffed grey hair; she shed tears of joy because Carter had finally married.

Carter introduced her as 'Valerie Falconer,' as they agreed she should keep her artistic name; Deborah interestingly remarked that now a days, women didn't have to change their names unless they wanted to. "It's a system that keeps us women so confused as to who we really are: only a man could have thought it up!" (Valerie was surprised by this robust opinion).

She felt a pull on the back of her skirt, so she stepped aside for Mercy to shake hands and say, "Good evening, Ma'am."

"Good evening, child!" Deborah apparently thought Mercy might be older than she was, because both her 'parents' were not young.

They sat at an old table with a beautifully woven tablecloth. Nate said a blessing in Hebrew. "That's a neat language," said Mercy. "I'd like to learn it someday."

"What did she say?" Nate asked.

"Dear, go and put in your hearing aids," said Deborah.

Once Nate had heard the remark, he replied, "Why some day, child? Start now. Our boys and girls do."

"Well, there's no place to learn it where I live."

"Mercy," said Carter "We can discuss this later."

Nate and Deborah looked at each other; they had both expected Valerie to more or less be the parent, with Carter following, but were further disappointed in their assumption when Mercy answered, "OK, Poppy." Then Mercy had a further request. "Great! And ma'am, could you show me how to make this chicken! It's so yummy!!"

"Mercy, "said her mother, "Stop there! Let's not overwhelm our hosts!"

"Ma'am," said Mercy, "Shall I take the plates out to the kitchen?"

"Is that your job at Pendragon?"

"Oh, we take turns. You see, Poppy was a bachelor for a long time and he knows how to do these things!"

Nate put the fingers of both hands against his forehead and began to laugh. Deborah put her head down on her arms crossed on the table, and was overcome with laughter.

The meal being over, Deborah suggested they move to the living room. As the table was left as was, Mercy dutifully took the plates out into the kitchen.

When she rejoined them, Mercy looked all around carefully and spotted a photograph of two young men tucked in a corner.

"Are these your kids?" she asked.

"Yes."

Her Poppy threw her a warning glance and she desisted.

"Nate," Carter said, "the Sidi gave me a photograph he told me you would probably understand."

"Let's see." Carter handed it to him, but Nate looked blank.

"Let me see," said Deborah. "Oh—Nate, it is El-Zeitoun."

"What is it?" Carter asked. Deborah asked them into her office and booted up her computer.

"You see, it is an apparition that appeared over a Coptic Catholic church at Zeitoun, Egypt. It was built by the Khalil family in the 11th century. It is the supposed site where Mary and Joseph lived when they fled into Egypt. For that reason, the Copts feel it is the cradle of Christianity.

"She manifested there over a three -year period from 1968-1972. First she healed a Moslem mechanic. Then the spot became a place where Moslems, Jews, and Christians all came together in peace."

"What interest do you believe this man has in this apparition?"

"It has been an interest since he was young."

"Could we meet him?"

“I’m sure we can arrange it.”

CHAPTER 18

Carter spoke to the Sidi about this request, and the latter was filled with enthusiasm. "I am eager to hear some of this man's knowledge!" the Sidi exclaimed.

Dinner was arranged, in consideration to Nate and Deborah, on a Sunday afternoon, so they would not have to stay up too late.

On Sunday, Carter and Valerie picked up Nate and Deborah and entered the Sidi's building on the ground floor, and into the elevator which whisked them two by two to the seventh floor. They stepped into a room which looked to them like the Arabian nights: it was Sidi's living room, heavily adorned in Arabian style; a large, expensive chandelier had pride of place hanging from the ceiling. The rugs had red backgrounds, swirling with carpeting designs. Biege couches surrounded three sides of the room, while the walls were a pale yellow, interrupted by red stripes. The curtains were a darker shade of yellow, trimmed in lighter yellow.

The walls were also hung with intricately designed symbols with beautiful frames; there were no paintings or photographs, in accord with the Moslem belief of no graven images such as photographs or paintings should be hung on walls.

The Sidi asked if his guests would prefer eating before or after talking. "I am afraid before!" said Nate.

"Let us go into my office. This is too formal a room for a good discussion." He led the way into a room with a desk and which had been set up with comfortable armchairs. There were pictures on the wall here, all of the same subject: our Lady of Zeitoun; for this reason, the Sidi kept his office door locked.

What was Sidi's idea? It was that Christians, Jews, and Moslems were all Children of Abraham.

"Admittedly," said Nate slowly. "What do you plan to do about it?"

"I am in contact with a rabbi and a monk who would be willing to go to the Mid-East with me, and travel from town to town to test the openness of citizens to the idea," said the Sidi.

"That is very bold, "said Nate. "even dangerous, I fear."

"I have always felt that when I aged, I should have to try to do something about it," said the Sidi. "I am not sure this is it, but at least it is a start. When you have seen the three faiths worshipping together, it forever haunts you."

"You are the one of the few who has probably seen it!" said Nate.

"Doubtless many others have, but not with the means to do something about it."

"What about your present activities?" asked Carter.

"Ah, Khalil and I have discussed this, and I will help him take over my role in our bunkering missions."

"Both Sidi and I will be stepping into new shoes," said Khalil.

"What do you plan to do about the devil?" asked Valerie.

"We shall be highly aware he would not approve our mission," answered the Sidi. "And, as we all share a concept of that evil being, we shall be triply armed! We lack agreement on a place to meet, however."

At this point, Deborah spoke up. "I think I may have an answer for you. This is why I brought this book with me." She produced a book with the title, *Sacred Spots of Britain.* "Walsingham is the oldest shrine in England, founded in 1061," she explained.

"Tell us about it."

"It was started by a religious woman named Richeldis de Faverches in 1061. She had a vision in a dream three times of a blueprint for Jesus' home in Nazareth, and a voice told her to keep the blueprint in mind, so she drew it the next morning. Workmen built it, but she did not know where to put it; they prepared two stone foundations, and the house was mysteriously moved 200 feet onto one of them. Because of it, England was called 'The Holy Land, Our Lady's Dowry.'

"It became a center for pilgrimages from everywhere. Many chapels were built on the way to it. One was called The Slipper Chapel, and it has been restored and still exists today. Henry the Eighth stopped there and walked the last mile barefoot in the snow. Then, of course, he established the church of England and razed it all to the ground. Today there is a new church, the Chapel, a mural from the Russian Orthodox church, as well as a monastery, a Methodist Church, and a very old Anglican church."

There was a silence around the table. It sounded ideal.

"I am sorry there is no synagogue there," said Deborah. "Or a mosque."

"Perhaps we may be able to build them. If not there, somewhere. In Jordan near Petra, a mosque and a church exist side by side," the Sidi informed them.

"I would be happy to be a consultant for your rabbi," said Nate. "He can hardly carry a library with him during the kind of travel you are describing. Here—I give you one of my cards. Deborah is on it too."

This agreed upon, they moved on to dinner. The table had been set in Western style, with wine for Carter and Valerie, kosher wine for Nate and Deborah and ice tea for the Sidi. The Arabs, Carter knew, took great pride in their hospitality, and indeed, everything was nearly perfect. Nate and Deborah enjoyed some of the fare, which was native to both the Sidi and Nate and Deborah's countries.

The Sidi tactfully seated himself in a Western dining room chair and asked Nate to say a blessing. His guest asked the Sidi, "English or Hebrew?"

"The latter," his host replied.

Carter and Valerie drove Nate and Deborah home; the two of them were exhausted from their stimulating visit. Then they returned and rode up to the tenth floor,

"Carter," Valerie said, "is Mercy bothering Deborah too much?"

"I think not. You see, they lost their two sons in Israel. That was the photograph in the living room. Deborah always gives it short shift. I have their wills and other papers in my safe. I have never looked at them. But, of course, they have no grandchildren."

"Oh!"

And it was thus Nate and Deboarh agreed to divide up their times with Mercy; Nate would tutor her in Hebrew, and Deborah would teach her to cook chicken.

Mercy had a comment that evening. "I'm not sure how to say something without sounding mean," she began to her parents.

"Then just say it."

"I like all the kids at school back home. They're fun to play with, but they're not too interested in school. Is there a nice school I could go to in London?"

"We are working on it, Mercy."

Working, indeed; all doors seemed shut, and they were contemplating the possibility of a commuter marriage, a contemplation that caused them both to be depressed, until a phone call informed them one school had a student drop out and there was an opening. It was, Valerie said, "an answered prayer!"

CHAPTER 19

One of the first things they knew they must do upon arrival is visit Adry and Brie at Pendragon. This of course, made them anxious, and they were half way through the drive when Mercy called a halt, saying that this is where they traditionally stopped to buy a candy bar.

"Come on, Poppy! This one is for you!"

"No thank you, Mercy."

"But it's good!" She had her stubborn look on her face.

I don't want to start a struggle. "All right, I'll try it."

Now they were on the final stretch, peeling off onto the dirt road which Pendragon maintained as it was so no local yabos would decide to race cars on it. Also, it was easier on the legs to jog on dirt rather than paving.

The cleaning lady met them at the door to tell them Adry and Brie were in the kitchen, having lunch. Now, Carter had eaten many meals in this house, but he had never seen the kitchen, so they descended the steps into it; it was partially built into a hillside, the other side with open windows. In the center was a large old wooden table, traditionally used for preparation. Straight to the rear were two Aga cookers, one red, and one black, and a sign that said 'Stendahl's corner.' On the black Aga, the cook usually cooked a lunch for their workers; on the red, the family supper. To one side was a large, open fireplace, big enough to roast an ox, with a modern spit installed. There were three refrigerators with temperatures registering on the doors, for meat, fish, and vegetables. Several drawers of old chests held cooking implements, and pots were hung along the walls. The cook said she would never work anywhere else.

Adry and Brie were seated at the table, having carved for themselves some ham for sandwiches. Adry jumped up to hug his mother. *Oh. Right, that's the American habit!* He thought. He shook hands with both of them.

The cook was bustling around, and gave each of them a sandwich. (She did not cook lunch for the family—or breakfast, either). Adry and Brie disappeared when they had finished theirs. Mercy finished hers and ran off the find her friends.

After lunch, Valerie mentioned looking in the storage for furniture, but Carter said there was one thing he wished to do first—visit Adrian's grave. "Shall I come with you?" She asked.

"No thank you, dear." He wanted to be alone. He knew he would cry.

He knew where he was going, and crossed diagonally, bending low under tree branches, until he came out to the left front side of the cemetery. All the tombstones were placed flat on the ground, for the family felt this was more gracious. Adrian was next to his parents, and Carter, overwhelmed, sat down on the grass beside the grave.

While I am down I may as well kneel, which he did, saying a short prayer. Then he sat again, knees up, with his arms circled around them, to contemplate the scene, which was, as usual, very peaceful, especially since it was the hour of the day when the birds stopped their singing.

He began speaking to his friend, first, needfully for Carter, explaining to him why he had missed his funeral. Moving along gradually, he told Adrian that he had married Valerie, and that they were taking Mercy with them. He hoped he had his friend's blessing: he also hoped he would be a help to the family. As he spoke, he felt a curious, almost trance-like sensation come over him, as if his world was touching another world. He had a strong sense of Adrian's presence that moved him to tears.

Then, faintly, he heard footfalls before the trees parted to reveal Adry. He sat down beside Carter; he had a scrapbook under his arm.

"I'm not sure on this, but perhaps you'd like to see several photos of Dad's funeral. Aunt Claudia took them. She said some had been taken at her father's funeral, and, although at first, they felt it was intrusive, several years later they were glad they had them."

"All right."

Adry opened the book to some back pages. Carter took the book.

Here were people he knew: Roulon and Mabel, Buddy and Karen, Charlie and Claudia. Workers from the business, relatives of the Falconers he did not know. Valerie on the arm of a man, clinging to him.

"Who is this?"

"Oh, that's Uncle George.

Her brother. The invisible one.

Why was it he had always had a picture in his mind of a spare group of people, to whom he might have added one more, which as well as making him distressed, made him guilty. As he looked at the sorrowful faces, it occurred to him how much Adrian was loved, and it comforted him. Slowly the guilt he had carried for the last three years lifted; people to whom Adrian meant a great deal were *there*. And now, he was glad that he, too, was there.

"Thank you, Adry," he said.

"You're welcome. I must admit I felt a bit of anger that you weren't there."

"I don't blame you."

They were silent for a few minutes. Then Carter asked, "Is this the brother who is always missing?"

"Why, yes."

"So many people. It is a tribute."

"Mom always says it's because Dad died young," said Adry with a smile.

The thought occurred to him now that he too, might be able to be buried here, and he felt an immense sense of gratitude. *I am not too late.* If that place beyond, is as it is described, was such, he would know

I am here today, as well as how upset I was not to be able to be there that day, all at once, in the ever-present.

"And you children—to have lost your father when you were so young." It was the first time an emotion other than his own had struck him. "Yes, and your grandma and grandpa too. I may be offensive, but the thought had occurred to me that these losses might make your mother lose her faith."

"It shook us all. But I have to say, Dad did a good job of inculcating us. In a way, I, myself, would have felt it would have been a betrayal to lose it."

"Now that I can see it that way, I understand."

"Mum said you'd been baptized in Texas."

"Yes, and it was not just to curry favor—as I suppose you might think."

"I must admit at first it did plague me how it ever occurred."

"Adry, I had a vision of the afterlife, and it scared me silly."

"Oh. Well, that makes sense."

"It's probably the best decision I've ever made."

More footsteps. Valerie hove into view. "Hello—Adry! Sorry, I didn't know you were here. Everything all right?"

She also sat down on the grass.

"Quite," said Adry. "Mom, what room shall we put the two of you in? Your old room?"

"That's OK."

Supper time found them at an old familiar spot, the local pub, O Give Thanks and Be Joyful. It had been Carter's way of expressing thanks by treating all of them to dinner there. Things tend to change slowly in the country, and Carter found it virtually unchanged: the same tables and chairs, bar and plates, and familiar faces. The owner, who always served as *maitre d'*, greeted them effusively and led them to their old table, which was, fortunately, empty. He seated the ladies, and handed them all menus. He exclaimed loudly, "Ah, Sir Carter! How nice to see you again!"

"Sorry," said Adry as they sat down. "He's just doing a bit of advertising."

Everyone opened their menus. "Thanks be," said Carter, "they haven't changed it."

"The old inferior fish debate," replied Adry, as if welcoming back an old friend.

"What's that?" Brie inquired.

"We always rode Carter about ordering plaice, because it is an inferior fish."

"It is not only inferior, it is inexpensive," Carter replied. "But I loved the way my mother cooked it. I've never tasted better. You see, I grew up in Clapham."

There was an awkward silence. Valerie finally said, "You see, Carter, they never knew that."

"Where's that, Poppy?" demanded Mercy.

"It was one of the poorer sections of London, Mercy. If you like, I will show it to you."

"Oh, yes!"

Adry, embarrassed, told Carter he now understood he had been rather rude.

"That's all right; I never wished to ruin a weekend with an experiential discourse."

"What was your Mummy like, Poppy?"

He leaned back in his chair. With a smile, he answered, "She made me the man I am today."

That night, about the middle of the night, Carter felt the mattress move in such a way as to indicate the other occupant of the bed had gotten up. *Probably off to the bathroom.* He rolled over, but a slight noise wakened him again. Where was she? Opening his eyes, he looked around the darkened room carefully.

There, at the window, one curtain was slightly lighter than the other, because Valerie was in front of it, looking out the window.

CHAPTER 20

When Carter arrived at chambers Monday morning, Ms.T. informed him they had inherited a new case which involved fraud and bribery.

"Why that? Why not the Fraud Division?"

"Usually, but this one is international. They've been lying in wait for you, Judge!"

Righto. No mercy.

He sat down to read and apprise it. *A British corporation seeking to minimize its taxes by funneling off some of their profits via France and Italy to Switzerland. No one had ever won a case against Switzerland. This will also take one of our solicitor's instructing. Do they have an anti-bribery policy? Operation shows a high degree of sophistication. Public interest: high. Tax evasion.*

"Do we have a review of the international companies?"

"Yes, C.P.S. has sent one over."

"There are the necessary translations?"

"Yes, Judge."

He spent the morning reading. *At least it looks to be something I can get my teeth into.* Occasionally Mercy's first day of school flitted through his mind. Carter settled in to what he felt might be a long process. When he finished reading the case over, he left for home.

He arrived at the fortress to find affairs in a state of discombobulation. Valerie had no idea of what time to order supper for she did not know when he would arrive home. Carter was unused to coming home to people. In the past, he could set his own schedule for supper and whatever else he wanted to do without interruption. "I'm sorry, I should have rung," he said.

"We'd better give each other blanket immunity on details for a while!"

"And how was your first day of school?" he asked Mercy, who appeared a bit downcast.

"Well, it was all new. I will have to catch up."

"That shouldn't be a problem."

"I don't know if the kids will like me. They think I'm—bucolic!"

"That you are. But you also have experience with something probably none of the rest of them have—a home in Texas!"

"The teacher says I should tell them something about me tomorrow."

"What's in your camera, Val?"

"Lots of photos of the ranch. One of a rattlesnake."

"I'm going to ask them downstairs to find an overnight developer." *That, I can do!* He should have known that the Sidi's operation had its own photo developer.

A large part of the rest of the evening was spent reminiscing about Texas, and helping Mercy collect her thoughts. At last, Mercy asked, "Oh, boy! What did you do today, Poppy?"

"I began to familiarize myself with a case the Crown Prosecution Service thinks we have a good chance of winning. It involves a British company here in England committing fraud and bribery. In this case, they are cheating on taxes. Initially, several individuals seemed to be carrying out these 'negotiations,' however, I suspect it goes deeper."

"Oh."

The next day, all of them, in varying degrees, wondered how her presentation went. She came home full of energy, which did not betoken failure.

"How did it go?"

"The first picture I showed was the rattlesnake. Some of the kids were scared! And the teacher didn't like it. But the kids really liked the pictures of grandpa roping cattle! They wanted to know how old he was, and why he had to rope cattle! When I told them about branding, some kids pitied the poor cattle."

"Oh."

He was upset when Valerie posited they should go back to Pendragon to look at their furniture collection, which they had not had time to do the weekend before. A repeat trip was not his definition of a weekend. Skulking wasn't manly, he decided, and tried to be cheerful.

However, Khalil called mid-week to see how they were coming.

"After all," his friend replied, "it is their home."

Khalil was right. They were leaving *their* home: Mercy, too, whom he had thought was an appendage to an adult. She was: but she was also herself. My two women.

"I would be pleased to meet Lady Val's family."

Carter instantly recalibrated. Khalil continued, "I will fly you there. It will save time, as well as you are still a guest under our roof!" Carter thought again before refusing. *Bedouin hospitality. Don't flout it.*

"By the way, Khalil has offered to fly us to Pendragon this weekend and I accepted."

He should have asked me. But I would have said yes anyway so does it really matter?

On Wednesday, there was a phone call, which MsT., as usual answered. "Judge, it is Lady Valerie," she announced. It was the first time his new life had intruded upon his old life, and he answered slowly, full of that first happening.

"Carter, I've found a rental we might like. Could you meet me after hours?"

Yes. He could. Valerie had found an unusual setting, a house set down in an old mews, with a skylight, and enclosed on both sides, on one by the small back yard of a house, on the other, an overgrown landscape. Inside, there was an eat -in kitchen, a living room, and a half bath on the ground floor. The first floor held two bedrooms, with a full bath in between. There was a second floor, which featured a storeroom with skylights, which had attracted Valerie's eye as good potential for a studio, and another room which could serve as a study for Carter. He decided to seize a chair in the kitchen with its back to the sink; his methodical self did not like the sight of unwashed pots, utensils, or plates. (He did not realize there was a dishwasher).

Mercy was accepting but unenthusiastic. She was a country girl, yet somehow, her living space had shrunk considerably. It struck her mother similarly, but a bit later. (Valerie was only used to visiting the city).

He was in a new old life: in Texas, he had been down home; here, he could himself becoming more pompous.

Later in the week, Valerie brought Mercy to Chambers again.

Mercy exclaimed, "Oooh, I love all the different colored books, don't you?"

"Unfortunately, Mercy, I cannot appreciate them because I am somewhat color blind."

"Ooo that's terrible! I will pray for you!"

No need to challenge childhood faith.

On Saturday, they left from the roof of the fortress and landed in the back of the house at Pendragon. Adry led them to the furniture repository; opening the door, it was revealed to be heated and dehumidified. Valerie was taken by a prodigious sofa, which Carter said would probably take up most of one wall; and, as he was an experienced mover, he measured it, and had the dimensions of the new rental with him. Valerie also unrolled an Oriental rug with a blue background which Carter was not sure was an Oriental rug, because, as Valerie told him, they do not all come in red and green; this one had a blue background.

This time, Mercy had not run off immediately to find her friends, as she was curious what was in the shed. She was allowed to pick out a chair. Valerie went off to a local upholsterer to pick out a fabric for the sofa. Adry invited Carter and Khalil down to see the new shop set-up now taking place. Carter could objectively appreciate the machinery whose use Adry described, but Khalil, who was more of a technical sort of man, had to examine each piece.

Then Adry asked Carter if he would like to see the books.

Not particularly. Count ten.

As he paused, he realized that this held some kind of superstitious ritual for Adry dating back to when he first read the books and determined the state of the business so many years ago. After all, Adry was a young man, starting up a business again, and a bit unsteady; probably wishing for the affirmation of his work from someone older—he had lost two generations of family men.

Only I remain.

"Very well, Adry; why don't you take Khalil to see Brie's workshop?"

Carter did not miss the look of relief that crossed his son-in-law's face.

Adry settled him at a desk with good light, and left with Khalil. Carter sighed, put on his glasses, and began to read. There was not yet much at this point, but it all seemed in order; what struck him was a list of repairs yet to be completed, under which was listed 'electricity.' Antiquated electricity. Not good. An inspector could put them out of business.

When Khalil and Adry returned, Carter asked Adry to walk with him. Khalil went over to the house. As they walked, Carter first affirmed that the books read well; then he tackled his worry, the electricity. It transpired it was Adry's worry, too.

What would Adrian want? The answer was clear.

"Call me a good electrical company, Adry, and send me the bill. After they are finished, of course, although they may require a retainer."

"Oh—you don't have to—"

"No, I don't, but this is now my family, too. And I shall worry if an inspector comes around, Adry!" *I am becoming a family man at the speed of lightening!*

Valerie had made a list of the desired furniture and handed it to Adry. Carter took it, scanned it, and said Adry was not to use a company truck to haul it; they would engage one.

As a result of Khalil's intervention, they were able to leave Pendragon by afternoon, arriving back in London. He was just about to settle down with the newspaper when Valerie announced they must visit a kitchen ware shop.

"We haven't any kitchen implements!" she announced. He decided that his presence was for added assurance and that he would pay the bill. Mercy dropped out, having been bored enough for one day.

Valerie dawdled around the shop, while he sat in a corner watching. He only sprang into action when she reached the counter to pay for her purchases—which she did, before he arrived. He announced that he would pay for that, but she asked, "Why?"

He could not think of an adequate response.

There was enough of it—pots and pans being bulky—to only carry some of it back to the fortress, and arrange for the rest of it to be delivered. Valerie asked Carter where he thought they should deliver it—to their new address? She arranged for the store to phone her before they delivered it, and she would meet them. They staggered home with bags of utensils.

Carter was surprised that doing something he would have found boring, was made enjoyable by doing it with his wife.

It's a whole new world.

He had never before particularly welcomed going to bed, but he did now.

After depositing them all in the fortress kitchen, Valerie lay down on one of the white sofas, and he sat on the other. He looked over and saw tears running down her face, without a sound. "Val, what is it?" he asked.

"Oh, nothing, I just feel exhausted, and can't carry on the way I used to."

She was too caring to mention Pendragon.

He got up and came over to her, handed her his handkerchief, and put his arm around her shoulder until she stopped crying, not saying anything.

CHAPTER 21

Carter's favorite hour was the one within the twenty-fours of the day when he was in bed with Valerie. It was dark and quiet in their own little world, made richer still by the mysterious spell a sleeping child casts over a house. When he first awoke during the night, he was not at first conscious of his new situation, yet when he was, he was thankful.

He surveyed the sleeping Valerie. His partner was right beside him, and earlier, they had made love. *I feel different. Could it be because I'm now legit?* Different bed, different man! She also appeared slightly confused, but that would fade, as would his. What a blessing to have a wife who also is my friend, and that he could often discern which was which.

The phone rang in his office. He rolled out of bed instead of letting it ring, as some sense of urgency overcame him. It was the Sidi. He apologized, and said he was airborne between Jordan and London. He had considered Deborah's suggestion of Walsingham as a good meeting place.

"Could you possibly travel with me there over the weekend?"

"What about Khalil?"

"I am leaving him in charge. It is in Norfolk. Can you meet me at North Liverpool Station?"

Despite the fact it was Saturday morning, and a good morning to sleep in, they got dressed in a state of excitement. When the train pulled in at North Liverpool Station, Valerie ran to catch an arrangement of a table between twin chairs on either side. The arrangement gave the Sidi enough room to stretch out his legs, as was Carter, Valerie giving preference to size.

"How are things with you?" asked the Sidi.

"We have made a pact to try never to be angry at the same time."

"An unusual starting point."

"I am used to arguing; Valerie is not."

Sidi said, with a smile, "If everyone in my household became angry at the same time, we would have a civil war!"

"May I ask how many wives you have? Is it offensive?"

"Not at all. I have four. That is the limit."

"Should I ask about children?"

"Twenty-five. My eldest son, Rashid, heads up our financial program. My children delight in discovering, for example, a shelf corporation formed in places—usually islands—to avoid paying taxes, or the tricks traders use to get orders in before anyone else by slow overnight messaging.

"You see, I am from an older generation which was dying out when I was young, when many marriages were of a political nature.

"There is a prophecy, I understand, about when Mary comes back to England," said the Sidi. "This strangely merges with Zeitoun. The Qu'ran reads, 'Oh, Mary, Allah has chosen you and purified you, and he has chosen you above all the world's women.'

"That does sounds portentous," said Valerie. "I know Protestantism claims that the gift of the Spirit died out with the Apostolic age, but once I met a Catholic priest from Ghana who was walking in the woods with his bishop and fellow priests, when they saw the dancing sun, just as it was at Fatima. Then he was sent to America. But they saw it again."

"Yes, mystery still exists," said Sidi with a smile. "I have seen it myself."

"Why is it you seem to spend a good deal of time with Christians??" Carter asked.

"Why does a salmon swim upstream?"

Meanwhile, life on the train went on around them. A woman bought a seat for her dog, who took occasional star turns up and down the train aisle, receiving pats and homage. He looked up expectantly at the Sidi, but the latter moved his hand to indicate this animal should move on. (Dogs are not particularly respected in some Arabian countries).

A man returning from the mid- East asked Valerie if they could watch his luggage while he used the loo. She was hesitant. Now passengers were on notice to report unwatched luggage. Could she refuse? What if there was a bomb in it? Would this involve a lack of trust in being asked to perform a charitable act? She shut down and waited.

At last, she saw the man returning.

At the train station in Norfolk, they found the usual offerings of sandwiches made by local households. They found a taxi for the rest of the journey, which would take an hour and a half.

"Where to, Guv?" the driver asked Carter, presuming that the Englishman had made the reservation.

"The Black Lion Inn," said the Sidi.

The village of Walsingham was somewhat underwhelming; it was small, with roughly cobblestoned streets and older style houses. At the inn, the road branched off into a pattern that constituted three sides of a square, allowing entry and egress from the fourth side. The inside walls of the inn were from a time when walls were not straight, but molded upward unevenly, made from mud reinforced with wooden beams, all painted white. It had a peaceable atmosphere. There was a small dining room on the ground floor, with one vegetarian plate. The Sidi and Valerie ordered it.

"My compliments to the chef," said the Sidi. "It is really quite tasty."

Several minutes later, the waitress came out of the kitchen with a young woman in a large white apron, pointing out the Sidi. That was going to be all, when the Sidi stood up, smiling. The waitress gave the chef a push toward him and she came up hesitantly. Only as she neared could Carter and Valerie perceive that the young woman was from the Mid -East. The Sidi began to speak to her in Arabic, and she broke out in a large smile. Carter and Valerie watched, entranced.

"I gave her my card. The fortress could use a good vegetarian cook."

When she had gone back to the kitchen, the Sidi returned and sat down. "There were a few different herbs in her cooking," he remarked.

Later, a bus stood by the front door, disgorging pilgrims from Liverpool with their priest, who displayed a fashion sense with a tan fedora and a tan jacket worn over his clericals. Although most of the pilgrims were older, and were staying at a pilgrims' hostel next door, there was a bar at one end of the inn where, later still in the evening (as their priest put it) they did what pilgrims do best: drinking beer and singing. It was an event they looked forward to all year.

In the morning, they walked down to the Anglican church, whose side chapels contained interesting painting or artwork, dating from centuries ago. On the way back, they noted a Methodist church. Then they walked in the opposite direction to the Anglican church, as far as a well which had been walled in with large, bluish tones arranged in a square. Sitting there was a monk.

Valerie commented that she thought he was a Franciscan, as he wore a brown habit.

The next day, they took the same walk, the only difference being that the monk was now joined by a rabbi with a yarmulke, and they were deep in conversation. On they went to the new Catholic church, which opened in the front to a bank of windows.

Carter wanted to go inside, but Valerie was hesitant, so the Sidi went with him. Later he said it was the best service he'd ever attended. There were three priests in their *soutanes* spread out across the long altar, standing in front of the bank of windows. As the Eucharist neared, suddenly, some Navy Harrier jets began to break the sound barrier overhead. A divine theophany! They never forgot it.

That evening, one of the villagers brought his eagle to show to the crowd. His owner wore a heavy leather glove, for its claws were fearful.

Nor did he have white head feathers like American eagles, but instead, his feathers were all one color.

"They were known to attack early airplanes! You can see how!" said Valerie.

Observed Carter, "Perhaps you should wear something like a robe or a head dress. I know those two chaps were looking you over today!"

"Yes, I also noticed."

Somehow, they all felt tonight was the last supper they would have together, and they lingered, and lingered, talking about Abraham. "Ibrahim," said the Sidi, "is considered to have an instinctive knowledge that there is only one God. Just as your religion superseded the religions of paganisms or naturalisms with Christianity, so our belief in the Hajj was taken into Islam through Abraham. We sacrifice a lamb on the last day of Hajj—somewhat similar to the Passover."

"Tell us why you complimented that young woman!"

"Muslims consider themselves a world community, and, we are instructed not to hoard our possessions but to use what we can to help others. We could use a good vegetarian cook."

"Do you think she might have thought of you…"

"As a procurer?" finished the Sidi. "I think not."

I think not either.

The next morning, with the Sidi more in character, the monk cried out, "Children of Abraham?"

"Children of Abraham." Before he walked over to them, he said, "Walk over with me. It will be good to have you meet these people."

As they came toward them, the two men stood up. The Sidi put his hands together made a short bow, and introduced himself. "And," he added, "these are my friends Carter and Valerie."

"Are they coming with us?"

"No, he is a judge," said the Sidi.

The monk, who, indeed, was a Franciscan, said to the Sidi, "your people and mine have been fighting forever!"

"Yes," said the Sidi, "save for several periods in Andalusia, and St. Francis." Brother Andrew nodded. They both knew what he meant.

Carter and Valerie were beginning to understand how much they did not know.

"You have not converted them?" Brother Andrew asked with a smile.

"I am free of guilt—I did not even try!" replied the Sidi with a laugh.

"Admirable," replied Brother Andrew.

Now attention turned to the Rabbi, who had been standing, listening, to the repartee. "Jacob Schmeer," he said, holding out his hand. The Sidi shook it.

There was a short discussion about transportation. No special cars or chauffeurs. Carter and Valerie watched the Sidi's expression. It was not altogether happy, but agreeable. They decided to summon a cab to take them to the train station.

Going back to the inn, the Sidi re-packed his small piece of luggage, while Carter used this brief time to go down and pay the bill. He gave a little smile of satisfaction.

A cab pulled up to the entrance, and the three men put their luggage in the boot. Carter and Valarie started to shake hands with them, while the Sidi gave them a hug.

Carter and Valerie walked along behind the taxi for a brief spell, for the cobblestones forced it to creep along. Finally, they came to the top of a small rise and stopped. They watched the car painstakingly descend down the cobblestone road, slowly vanishing.

www.ingramcontent.com/pod-product-compliance
Lightning Source LLC
Chambersburg PA
CBHW031752200726
48289CB00013B/865